Celia and the FAIRIES

Karen McQuestion

two lions

two lions

Text copyright ©2010 Karen McQuestion
All rights reserved
Printed in the United States of America

This book was published, in a slightly different form, in 2009.

Published by Amazon Publishing
Attn: Amazon Children's Publishing
P.O. Box 400818
Las Vegas, NV 89140

ISBN-13: 9781935597285
ISBN-10: 1935597280

For my goddaughter, Josie

CHAPTER ONE

*E*very night after Celia was tucked into bed, she tiptoed out of her room and sat quietly on the upstairs landing. Listening, always listening. If she was very quiet she could hear her parents' voices from below. Most of the time their conversations were boring, but every now and then she heard something important.

So when her mother and father called her into the living room for a big announcement one day, she already knew what they were going to say. They motioned for her to sit down, and then her mother began. "As you know, Celia, Grammy has been living with Aunt Joanne since you were a baby."

Dad leaned forward, elbows resting on his knees. "Just recently Aunt Joanne accepted a new job overseas. She'll be selling her condo and moving to France."

"So it's been decided," Mom said, "that Grammy will come to live with us."

Dad added, "She'll use the downstairs bedroom. Our lives will basically be the same, except that your grandmother will be part of everything we do. Do you understand?"

Celia understood more than they knew. "I think it will be nice to have Grammy here." In truth, she was deliriously happy with this new development. Her grandmother was one of her favorite people in all the world. Grammy had a ready laugh, always listened, and never pried. Best of all, Grammy clearly adored her. Really, Celia could do no wrong in her grandmother's eyes.

Her parents looked pleased at her response. They thought she was an especially insightful child. "Wise beyond her years," her father was fond of saying. "Just like talking to an adult," her mother often said. "It's because we don't baby her," they both agreed, taking credit for her maturity.

Her mother smiled. "Your Aunt Joanne will be bringing Grammy on Sunday. This isn't a visit. She'll be staying with us for a long, long time." She'd overheard her parents discuss this at length. They'd said, "We must make sure Celia understands that this isn't short term, or there will be problems."

Celia nodded thoughtfully, to show she understood.

"We'll be relying on you to help Grammy," her father said. "This will be a difficult change for her. She'll need help finding things around the house, especially in the kitchen. And one more thing." He stopped to look at her mother, who gave him an encouraging nod. "Your grandmother might tell you stories about magical things in the woods behind our house. It was a story she used to tell me when I was a child, just a made-up story. Lately, for some reason, she's been insisting it's true."

"Luckily," her mother added, "you're old enough to know there is no such thing as magic. Be kind and agree with her, but remember what we've said. We'll need to watch out for

Grammy. Your father and I know we can count on you to help."

"What kind of magical things?" Celia asked.

Her father waved his hand dismissively. "Nothing you need to worry about. Just a lot of nonsense."

"It might not even come up," Mom said. "We just wanted to mention it in case it did." She gave Celia a firm look to let her know the subject was closed. "Do you have any more questions about Grammy coming to live with us?"

"Does this mean," Celia asked, "that I don't have to go to Paul's after school?" She knew the answer was yes, of course, but thought she'd mention it while they were on the subject. She and Paul were the last two drop-offs on their bus route. They'd been best friends when they were younger, but now Paul, who was a year younger and a grade behind her in school, was starting to get on her nerves. There wasn't much left of the school year, and she'd had her fill of being bossed around.

Maybe it was because she'd gone to his house every day after school since kindergarten. Her parents worked long hours at the company they owned. Lovejoy World was a business that made traditional toys and board games. Their products were environmentally friendly and had won many awards.

The company's motto was the phrase "Bring back family time!" printed beneath a sketch of a family sitting around the table playing *Trixie-Dixie: The Good Deed Game*, something her father had invented. It was voted America's most beloved board game for children under twelve, and Celia loved to play it, but Paul was never interested, insisting they pretend to be army spies or ninjas instead. He got to pick the games, he said, because it was his house, and he thought *The Good Deed Game* was stupid.

"Yes," said her mother. "You won't have to go to Paul's house anymore. You can get off the bus right here at home and stay with your grandmother until your father or I get back from work."

Celia thought about how nice it would be not to have to go to Paul's and said, "I think this will work out just fine."

CHAPTER TWO

When her aunt and grandmother arrived that Sunday, Celia was sent to help Grammy unpack, while the other adults—her parents and Aunt Joanne—went over "important details" in the living room. Celia was glad not to be part of that discussion. She already knew what it would be about: medication and eyeglasses and money. Nothing she cared about. It would be more interesting to see what Grammy pulled out of her suitcases.

"Is this all you have?" Celia asked, helping to lift three suitcases onto the bed.

"When you get to be my age, you don't need very much." Grammy smiled and rested a hand on Celia's forehead, like she was checking for fever. Her grandmother's skin felt warm and smelled like the baby powder Celia's mother sprinkled in her running shoes.

The first suitcase was all clothing. Celia helped put things on hangers, while her grandmother put nightgowns, socks, and underwear into dresser drawers. The next two suitcases contained what Grandmother called "personal items." She had books and a pillow, cut-glass bottles of perfume, a jewelry box filled with treasures, and framed family photographs. While Celia unwrapped the paper from each breakable item, Grandmother arranged the pictures on the top of the long, flat dresser.

Celia recognized most of the photos. There was one of her father and Aunt Joanne as children taken on the front porch of their house, the very same house she lived in now. Both of them wore cowboy hats and fringed vests. Another picture showed Grammy and her husband on their wedding day. Both of them were *very* skinny and *very* young, so different from being old (Grammy) and dead (the grandfather she'd never met).

Grandmother held up a photo Celia hadn't seen before. "Do you know who this little girl is?"

Celia studied it carefully. The girl in the black-and-white photo looked just like her, but it wasn't her. Certainly she'd never worn her hair pulled up to one side with a bow perched on top, like an enormous butterfly. But the face was definitely what she saw in the mirror each morning—pale skin, freckled nose, and a dimple in one cheek. Her mother said Celia had a heart-shaped face, which was supposed to be a good thing. Puzzled, Celia shook her head.

"You can't figure it out?" Grammy asked. "This is a photo of me, when I was about your age."

Celia took the photo from Grammy's hand to get a closer look. "It looks just like me."

"Yes, they named you well when they gave you my name," Grandmother said. "Old Celia and young Celia, that's us."

Celia was glad she got to be the younger version. She secretly thought it must be so sad to be Grammy and have white hair and skin like crepe paper.

"I don't mind being old," Grandmother said, interrupting her thoughts. "I've had many adventures in my life. You'll be lucky if you live as long and as well as I have." Celia nodded politely. "And my very first big adventure happened to my sister and me when I was just about your age. Would you like to hear about it?"

And Celia said she would.

CHAPTER THREE

*W*hile Grammy was telling her story, a group of fairies gathered in the woods behind Celia's house.

Mira, the leader of the Watchful Woods fairies, took her job very seriously. Unfortunately, the rest of the group didn't always cooperate. "Attention, everyone, attention!" she said, once all the fairies had met in the clearing. "I have news." She waited for complete silence, but a few in the back kept whispering, so she clapped her hands together twice and switched to her *no-nonsense* voice. "Quiet, everyone, this is important." Everyone hushed then, except the twins, Trixie and Dixie, who continued chattering to each other. So typical. Now Trixie was flitting up in the air admiring her sister's headband, a crown of flowers.

Mira sighed. The twins were such bubbleheads, never able to take anything seriously. Probably because they didn't have a real responsibility. Instead of being assigned a family like the rest of them, they were in charge of good deeds for the area. They flitted from house to house, silently urging people to do good deeds. Their biggest accomplishment was getting Jonathan Lovejoy to invent *The Good Deed Game*. After the game became big, they were impossible to live with. Community activists, they called themselves, and took credit for every good deed done anywhere in the world. As if one game could make that much difference. "Ladies!" Mira yelled. "Settle down."

Trixie plunked herself down with a dramatic bounce and flapped her wings a few times for emphasis. "Okay, Mira, don't have a breakdown."

Mira cleared her throat. "I have important news. Celia, the original Celia, has moved back to the Lovejoy house." There was a moment of stunned silence before the fairies started talking all at once.

"The original Celia is back?"

"When did this happen?"

"Does this mean what I think it does?"

"Is the game in danger?" This from Dixie, who was always thinking of herself and her sister before anything else.

Mira held up a hand. "Quiet, everyone. I'm not sure yet what it means. I just want you all to be aware that Celia is back, and I feel a change coming on. Something is going to happen. We have to be on our toes." She turned to one fairy boy. "Especially you, Boyd, because you're in charge of the other house. What's the name of the boy there?"

Boyd ran a hand through his curly hair and squinted. "Peter? No wait, that's not it. Paul, I think."

"Do you think, or do you know?" Mira was critical of fairies who didn't do their jobs, and Boyd was the worst of these. A total slacker.

Boyd slouched back against a rock. "Yes. No. I mean, I'm pretty sure his name is Paul."

"Keep an extra close watch, then, on Paul and his parents," Mira said. "Whenever something happens in one house, it's connected to the other one. You must be extra vigilant."

"Sure, okay," Boyd said with a yawn. "I'm on it. You can count on me."

⁎

CHAPTER FOUR

*G*rammy settled into the armchair next to the bed, while Celia sat at her feet. "My sister Josie was two years older than me. We grew up in this exact house, and we shared the bedroom upstairs in the back. The room with the balcony."

"That's my room," Celia said, pleased. She loved her house with its built-in bookcases, winding staircase, and two cozy fireplaces; and she especially loved her room with the french doors leading outside. She was the only one in her grade to have her own balcony.

Grandmother nodded and continued. "I remember the exact day because it was Easter Sunday. That evening we saw something very special, something that changed my life forever.

"Springtime that year was especially warm, just like it is now. My parents had invited all the relatives and a few family friends over for Easter dinner. Our little house was full of people and laughter and song. Mama's cooking smelled like heaven. I can still taste her glazed ham and potatoes. Nobody could cook like her.

"And there was music! We used to have a piano in the front room, and someone was always playing, and we all sang along. Holidays were always so lovely, a good reason to have a party. Josie and I got to stay up later than usual that night, but eventually Papa said we had to go up to bed. Back then, children never argued with their parents, so up we went without a word."

Grandmother smiled down at Celia. "We weren't as good as all that, though, because once we'd changed out of our day clothes, we stayed up and spied on the adults. The holiday party had moved outdoors onto the back patio, and that night Josie and I crept out onto the balcony to watch and listen. I remember that we had on matching long nightgowns, the kind with a ruffle at the bottom. My mother had made them, and we loved wearing them. The material was so soft and full; it floated when we spun around. Girls don't wear nightgowns like that anymore, I don't think.

"Anyway, we sat on the balcony cross-legged, listening to the grown-ups talking, and I was getting sleepy. Suddenly Josie grabbed my arm and whispered, 'Look, Celia, fireflies!' She pointed and I saw it, too: dozens of the biggest fireflies I'd ever seen were flitting around in the woods just beyond the patio.

"The grown-ups didn't notice, but we kept our eyes on them, mesmerized. I wasn't tired anymore. Eventually the patio crowd drifted back into the house, and we were able to move closer to the edge of the balcony. We stood on our tiptoes and leaned over the railing as far as we could. That was when Josie said, 'They can't be fireflies, Celia. It's too early in the season. I think they're fairies.'"

Grandmother, looking off in the distance, was too busy telling the story to notice Celia's eyes grow wide in amazement. "Now Josie sometimes tried to fool me. She'd tell me monster stories at night when we were lying in bed. Other times, when we were alone in the house, she told me fanciful tales of ghosts that haunted our cellar, or mermaids that lived in the creek in the back. When I was much smaller I believed her, but by the time I was ten I wasn't so easy to trick.

"But there was something about these lights that didn't seem like ordinary fireflies. And standing there on the balcony, concentrating as hard as I could, it seemed as if I could almost make out the outline of each fairy by the glow of her light. If I really looked hard, I saw their wings, sheer as a dragonfly's, and their slender arms and legs. The longer I looked, the more it seemed possible. I said to Josie, 'Do you really think they could be fairies?' and before she could answer, one flew up as gracefully as a ballerina and appeared right in front of our eyes. I saw her clearly, her face just like a human girl's, her wings fluttering as quickly as a hummingbird's, her dress shimmering like silk. I think she was as curious about us as we were about her. It was just for a moment, one beautiful glowing moment, and then whoosh—she was gone. I'm an old lady now, but I remember that moment as clearly as if it were yesterday."

CHAPTER FIVE

*G*randmother's story was interrupted by a knock on the door—Celia's father telling them dinner was ready. Drat! Such poor timing. Celia would have skipped the meal to hear the rest of the story, but that wasn't an option, unfortunately.

Dinner that night was pot roast: chunks of beef swimming in gravy with mushy carrots, onions, and potatoes. Pot roast wasn't Celia's favorite, not even close, but there were also biscuits with butter, so she filled up on those. Aunt Joanne and Grandmother raved about the food, and between the compliments and the passing of dishes, no one paid much attention to Celia until Aunt Joanne set down her fork and said, very brightly, "Celia!"

Pulled out of her thoughts, Celia looked up, startled.

"Celia," she repeated, "a little bird told me that you are pleased to have your grandmother come live with you? Is that true?" Aunt Joanne had no children of her own and always spoke to Celia in a weirdly formal way. Whenever she asked something, it sounded like a trick question.

"Yes," Celia said. "I'm very glad she's here." Especially since having Grammy live with them meant Celia could come straight home after school. During vacations Celia went to work with her parents, and that was never a problem. She loved going to Lovejoy World, where the older ladies fussed over her and young J.J. let her help with his cleaning duties, but on school days she had been stuck going to Paul's. Bossy old Paul, who always had to have things *his* way. No more of that.

"The two of you should get along well," Aunt Joanne said patting Grammy's arm. "Your grandmother loves to bake and go for walks. And you can tell her all about what happens at school. She's an excellent listener. She'd probably love to hear stories about what you're learning in class."

"Grammy is good at telling stories, too," Celia said. "Before dinner she told me about a time she and her sister thought they saw fairies."

Grammy smiled, but the other adults looked alarmed. Celia's hand flew up to her mouth, as if to take back the words, but it was too late. She could tell she'd gotten her grandmother in trouble. Oh, why didn't she think before she spoke?

"Oh no," Aunt Joanne said, groaning.

"Mother, please tell me you didn't share that story with Celia," Dad said. It was a foolish thing for him to say, because of course she had—isn't that what Celia just said? "I thought we agreed not to talk about that anymore." His mouth was half open, making his face look long.

"I like hearing stories about the olden days," Celia said, defending her grandmother. "I learned all kinds of things, like no one ever told me that Grammy and her sister used to have the same bedroom as me."

"Talking about the olden days is one thing," Dad said, with an unconvincing smile, "but I don't think we need to bring up that fairy business again." He turned to Grammy. "We've always believed children should know the truth about everything, and that is how we've raised our daughter. Celia has known from the start that there is no tooth fairy, no Easter bunny, and certainly no such thing as ghosts or elves or fairies."

Mom joined in. "We have nothing against other people spinning such tales, if that's what they think is best, but we believe in truthfulness. The world is a beautiful, wonderful place. Every sunrise and butterfly is a miracle to us, so we don't feel the need to make things up. If you tell Celia the fairy story and don't explain that it was all in your imagination, she might think it was real and become disappointed when she finds out the truth."

"You can think what you want. Celia is old enough to hear the facts and decide for herself," Grammy said. "I'm only telling her what happened to me."

"Really, Mother," Aunt Joanne said. "You can't tell me you believe you saw fairies! I know you thought so at the time, but you were just a child then. Be sensible. You don't want to go putting nonsense in Celia's head."

"Say what you want. I know what I saw." Grammy calmly speared a chunk of carrot with her fork. "I wouldn't worry too much about Celia, if I were you. I can tell she has a mind of her own." She took a bite, winked at Celia, and then addressed Celia's mother. "I know I said it before, Michelle, but this dinner is just delicious. I would love to have your recipe."

That night, when Celia's mother came up to her bedroom to say good night, the subject surfaced again. "Remember how we said your grandmother might tell you stories about magical things?" Mom said, adjusting the covers so they lined up perfectly. "Well," she continued, "this fairy business is what we were talking about. Obviously fairies aren't real. I'm sure I don't need to tell you that. If your grandmother insists on talking about it, just play along. We love Grammy and don't want to upset her. Think of it as a very nice story, but remember that it's just that—a story, okay?"

To be agreeable, Celia said okay, but after her mother shut off the lamp, turned on the nightlight, and closed the door, she got out of bed and peered out the window into the darkness. She stared for the longest time, trying to imagine what her grandmother and her sister had seen in the woods beyond the patio so long ago. And just as she turned to go back to bed, she thought she saw one small wink of light, just a quick flash, and then it was gone.

Later on she couldn't be sure she saw anything at all.

CHAPTER SIX

On the bus ride home from school the next day, Paul insisted on sitting right next to Celia, even after everyone else got off and they were the last two left. "My mom said she was gonna buy batteries for my walkie-talkies today. And I have that spy kit with all the cool stuff for fingerprinting and seeing in the dark," he said, his voice ending in a screech. "When we get to my house, we can go out in the woods and play that we're spies." He bounced in the seat like his butt was on springs.

Celia looked out the window and sighed. "I told you, Paul," she said impatiently. "I'm not coming over after school anymore. My grandmother lives with us now, so I don't need to go to your house."

"But you're going to come sometimes, right?" He rested his feet on the seat in front of them. "Because we're still working on the LEGO castle, remember? We still have to do the drawbridge and all the other stuff. Right? We can't stop now. We're almost done."

Celia's house came into sight as the bus turned the corner onto her road. "You can go ahead and finish the castle without me," she said, picking up her backpack. "I won't be able to come over for a long time. My grandmother needs me at home."

"How long is your grandma going to live with you?" he asked. "Not too long, I hope. Maybe she'll die or go off to Florida like my grandma did."

"My Grammy is *not* going to die, and she's not going to Florida. She's going to live with us for years and years and years, and she needs me to be with her when I get off school. I told you that already, Paul."

As the bus came to a stop, Paul stood up to let Celia get past. "Maybe next week you could come over and play?"

"I don't think so," she said, getting up to make her way to the front. As the bus driver pulled on the lever and the doors whooshed open, she turned to wave to Paul. His sad face made her feel a little guilty, and it occurred to her that maybe she could invite him to *her* house. The only problem with that was that she didn't really want him there because she liked having her grandmother all to herself. Finally she said, "See you tomorrow, Paul."

Celia stepped down from the bus and headed up the walkway toward home. "Hello, Celia," Grammy said, smiling as she held the door open. "How was your day?" A good smell welcomed her from inside. Something chocolatey. This was so different from Paul's house, where the only greeting was his mother saying wearily, "Are you kids here already?" Sometimes Paul's mother was napping when they arrived, and they had to use the key under the mat to get into the house. On those days they had to be very quiet because she had a headache.

"My day was good," Celia said, shaking off her backpack and dropping it on the mat by the door.

Ten minutes later, Grammy and Celia sat at the kitchen table, each with a glass of milk and a large brownie topped with vanilla ice cream. At Paul's house, Celia usually had carrot sticks or pretzels with water.

Grammy was a good listener. In between bites Celia told her about her day at school. There'd been a drama in her classroom when one of the boys reported money missing from his desk. At lunchtime, the cafeteria served crusty fish sticks with tartar sauce as thick as paste. Celia hadn't eaten much of it. "And in the afternoon, we went to the computer lab and played basketball in gym class. That was fun."

"You're lucky." Grammy swirled the ice cream with her spoon. "We didn't have computers or basketball in school when I was your age."

"But you saw a fairy when you were the same age as me." Celia met her grandmother's eyes questioningly. Would she deny it? Say that it had been just a made-up story?

"Yes," her grandmother said. "I did see a fairy. In fact, I saw a whole world of fairies. They lived in the woods behind this house. Would you like to hear the rest of the story?"

CHAPTER SEVEN

*G*rammy set her spoon down and smiled at Celia. "I think I mentioned that the first time I saw the fairy girl was on Easter Sunday. She flew right up to us, and then was gone lickety-split. After that, Josie and I started looking for fairies. Every night after our parents tucked us in, we sneaked out of bed and sat on the balcony watching the woods for signs. Night after night we watched and waited, but we didn't see anything. After two weeks or so, we started doubting ourselves. Had we really seen a fairy?"

"What else would it have been?" Celia asked.

Her grandmother shrugged. "We didn't know. A bird, a dragonfly, a firefly? None of those seemed likely. We wondered if we'd dreamt the whole thing or maybe just imagined it. Josie really lost hope we'd ever see one again, but I was sure we would. In fact, I knew it."

"How did you know?"

Grammy leaned in toward Celia. "I dreamt about her. I saw her over and over again in my sleep. She had pale skin and bright eyes and wings as sheer as my mother's stockings.

Sometimes in my dreams she sang so beautifully I still remembered the sound of it when I woke up. I thought she was trying to send me a message. Josie thought I was being silly and wouldn't listen to my talk about dreams. Big sisters are like that sometimes. She felt superior because she was older."

Celia remembered that she'd felt that way about Paul and decided she'd be extra nice to him the next time she saw him. It wasn't his fault she'd outgrown his games. "So then what happened?"

"One night we were out on the balcony watching, and Josie got tired and went back inside. I'm not sure what made me stay out there all by myself. I just had a feeling I should wait a bit longer. And that's when it happened.

"There was a rustling in the woods, like a large animal tearing through the brush. A dog, I thought. I stood up then and leaned over the railing to see if I could get a better look. A spring breeze whipped at my nightgown, and I kept hearing noises like twigs breaking and something moving low to the ground. Then the night air was pierced by a scream that went right through me. It made the hair on the back of my neck stand up.

"The scream wasn't anything I could hear with my ears—it was only in my head. It came straight into my mind, just like the fairy girl's singing in my dream. I could tell it came from the direction of the woods."

"So what did you do?"

"I didn't know what to do at first. I was frozen in place. It was probably only a minute, but it felt like hours." Grammy shook her head. "Like being trapped in a nightmare."

Celia nodded. She knew what that was like. When she was little, she'd had bad dreams of being cornered by wart-covered monsters with long claws and sharp fangs. Other times she'd dreamt about being held underwater and not being able to breathe, or getting lost and trying frantically to get home. Even now, if she had a nightmare she some-times woke up her mother for reassurance. Night terrors always seemed so real in the dark.

"And then I saw a glimmer of light off in the distance, and I heard the fairy's voice in my head, begging me to come, that they needed my help."

"She knew your name?"

Grammy nodded. "'Celia, please help!' is what I heard. She was begging me, calling my name over and over again. I couldn't ignore it."

"So you went into the woods?" Celia whispered.

"I did." The telephone rang just then, and they each turned toward the noise. "I better get that," Grammy said, reluctantly getting up from the table. "It might be your parents."

It was Celia's parents—she could tell from listening to her grandmother's half of the conversation. When Grammy returned to the table, she said, "Your parents are going to be a little late tonight. They have an important meeting with Vicky McClutchy."

Oh, that again. Celia had heard her parents talk about this many times. Vicky McClutchy was the owner of McClutchy Toys. She wanted to buy her parents' toy com-pany and had approached them several times, but Celia's father wasn't interested. He didn't like Vicky McClutchy, and he didn't like the idea of someone else owning his creations, especially *Trixie-Dixie: The Good Deed Game*, his pride and joy. He never tired of telling people that he got the idea in a dream. "If that Vicky McClutchy gets a hold of it, she'll use cheaper materials and junk it up," he said, running his hands through his hair. "And change it all around. Eventually she'll turn it into some kind of horrible video game. It just wouldn't be right."

Celia's mother was a little more open-minded. "We can at least listen to what she has to say," she said. "For that kind of money, we could retire early and still have plenty for Celia's college fund."

"I will never sell my soul for cash," was how her father responded. Her mother thought he was being a little dramatic.

For all her parents' talk, they'd never actually had a business meeting with Vicky McClutchy until now. It looked like Celia's mother had finally gotten her way. "Anyhow," Grammy said, "I guess it will be just you and me for a bit. Now where were we in the story?"

"The fairy girl called for help," Celia prompted. "And you went."

"Oh yes." Her grandmother smiled. "Would you mind if we moved into the living room first? The chairs in there are kinder to my back."

CHAPTER EIGHT

*G*rammy smoothed her skirt as she settled back onto the green sofa. Celia sat next to her and hugged a throw pillow.

"I think," Grammy said, "that I was just getting to the part where the fairy girl was calling for my help, wasn't I?"

Celia nodded. "You couldn't ignore her, you said. You just *had* to go."

"That's right," her grandmother said. "I went into the bedroom to wake up Josie, but she was sound asleep and wouldn't budge. I thought I might be able to sneak past my parents and slip out the back door, but when I went to the stairs I heard them in the living room and knew that wouldn't work. They would have seen me. But I knew I had to get to the woods. It was a matter of life or death. So I climbed over the balcony railing and shimmied down the vines to the ground—"

"You did what?!"

Grammy smiled. "I was like you then, young and limber. And those vines are quite strong. Josie and I used to climb down them all the time. We used the brick for footholds and held onto the vines like rope."

This was a new idea to Celia, who would never have thought to try such a thing. How shocking to think that olden-days girls would be so daring. When she'd thought of her grandmother and great-aunt as children, she'd imagined them knitting, not rappelling down the back of her house. And to leave the house by yourself, in the dark? Unthinkable. Once at Paul's they'd been playing in his basement when he suddenly ran up the stairs and turned off the lights, leaving her in the pitch black. He'd thought it was funny, but she panicked and screamed until he turned the light back on. "Don't be such a baby," Paul had said, in a mean voice. After that he was extra nice to her so she wouldn't tell his mother, but she never forgot. Now, even thinking about being alone in the dark made her heart race and gave her breathing problems.

"Don't tell your parents I used to climb down the vines, or they'll think I'm giving you bad ideas." Grandmother lifted a finger to her lips. "Promise?"

"I promise."

"So I climbed down as fast as I could. There was a full moon that night, so everything was well lit, until I entered the woods. I was still in my nightgown and the ground was wet against my feet, but I went quickly, following the noise and the glimmer of light."

Celia moved closer to her grandmother, anxious to take in every word.

"I heard the fairy girl calling my name over and over again. I shouted, 'I'm coming,' and I kept going. I'd never been out by myself at night before. My heart was beating so loudly I felt it in my throat. When I finally reached the light ahead of me in a clearing, it took a second for my eyes to adjust.

"What I saw sent chills through me. A fairy girl was snagged on a thorn bush, cornered by a fierce-looking coyote. The animal had his teeth bared and was growling deep in his throat. He was crouched like he was about to attack, and she was twisting and turning, trying to free herself.

"I could tell it was the same girl I'd come face-to-face with on the balcony. She had a soft glow around her, like she was lit up from somewhere inside of her. When I stepped into the clearing, the coyote turned his attention away from her and snarled in my direction."

"Were you afraid?" Celia asked.

Her grandmother nodded. "I felt like throwing up, if you must know. Either that or running away, but I thought if I ran, the coyote would come after me and attack."

Celia said, "My father says coyotes don't usually bother humans. That they're more afraid of us than we are of them."

"That's normally true," Grandmother said. "But this wasn't a regular coyote. This one was actually a shadow thing in disguise."

"What's a shadow thing?" Celia asked, snuggling closer to her grandmother.

"I'm so very glad you asked," Grammy said, smiling. "I'm one of the few people in the world who knows the answer to that, and now I'm going to tell you. It's a secret that I've kept mostly to myself. The few people I've told thought I was joking or crazy, so after a while I learned to keep quiet about it." She looked up at the ceiling and sighed. "To answer your question, a shadow thing is a creature who stirs up bad energy and tries to influence what people say and do. They want people to steal and cheat and lie because then they can feed off the evil. They love greed and selfishness because those two things are the roots of human conflicts. We people live our lives going to work and school, doing all the things we do, never knowing that under the surface there are forces of good and evil at work. It affects everyone and everything."

Celia felt her throat tighten. "Isn't there anything we can do about the shadow things?"

Her grandmother smiled. "Every day when we make the right choices we defeat them. Every time you get an idea to do something you shouldn't, whether it's to say a mean thing or cheat on a test, and then you don't do it because you know it's wrong, you've battled the evil and won. People are more powerful than they know."

"But sometimes the shadow things win?"

"Yes, sometimes they win. They prey on people when they're at their weakest, confused and tired and depressed. That's when we sometimes get help from fairies and other good spirits."

"What can the good spirits do?"

"The good spirits try to help us and guide us to do what is right. That's why dark things are always trying to destroy fairies. And that's why the dark thing, disguised as a coyote, wanted to destroy Mira."

"Mira—that was the fairy's name?" Celia asked.

Grammy said, "Yes, that was her name. It was Mira who came up to us on the balcony the first night, and she was also the one cornered by the shadow thing. I didn't know it was a shadow thing at the time, though. They're very good at taking other forms and disguising themselves. I thought it was a rabid coyote. When I first saw it I was shaking with fright, but when Mira turned to me and I saw how she was counting on me, I forgot my fear and got a surge of strength. I picked up a stick off the ground and waved it at the thing and started yelling at it to go away."

"And it ran off then?"

"No, but it backed up a little bit, growling and snapping its teeth the whole time. I was able to get closer to Mira. I kept yelling and waving my stick with one hand, and with the other hand I was able to free her from the thorn-bush. Once she was loose she flew up in the air, fluttered her wings, and made this wonderful noise to call the other fairies. I can't describe the sound exactly, but it was kind of like..." Grammy looked up dreamily. "Like a mixture of a symphony playing and beautiful singing. Like the most wonderful music you've ever heard. It filled me with such joy." She looked down at Celia. "Have you ever heard anything like that?"

Celia thought for a moment. "I don't think so."

Grandmother sighed. "It's a shame. No one else I know has ever heard it either. So beautiful, like a noise from heaven. Anyway, Mira was calling her friends, and before I knew it, I was surrounded by fairies, dozens of them. The light they gave off was so bright it lit up the woods. I saw the coyote explode into dust particles and get sucked off into the darkness."

"It just disappeared?" Celia asked, amazed. "How come?"

"It couldn't stand to be in the presence of so many light beings. Shadow things thrive on negativity, and fairies are just the opposite. They're here on earth to do good. That's why the shadow thing was trying to kill Mira."

"What happened next?"

"The fairies hovered around me with their wings fluttering and their lights glowing. They were so curious about me. It's not often they get so close to a human. Their little voices were chattering away. I could just barely make out what they were saying. Mira had a close call, they said. She shouldn't have been out by herself at night. They said she was lucky I'd come to help, but they were worried now that I would tell people about them and where they lived in the Watchful Woods."

Putting her arm around Celia, she added, "That's what they call the woods behind this house—the Watchful Woods. Anyway, when I arrived on the scene, they didn't know what to make of me. Very few people can actually see them, and the fairies like it that way. They value their privacy, you know. Fairy work requires complete secrecy."

Celia nodded, even though she was a little unclear on what work her grandmother meant.

"I assured them I could keep a secret," Grammy said. "I promised not to tell a living soul, and for the most part I kept my promise." She sighed happily. "Anyway, that first night they took a vote and decided I was trustworthy. They can read people, you know. They look right into your heart."

"Were you afraid?" Celia looked up and met Grammy's twinkling eyes.

Her grandmother shook her head. "No, I wasn't afraid. I was fascinated, if you want to know the truth of the matter. After they told me I could go, I got the notion to hold out my hand like this," she said, stretching her arm out, palm up, "and Mira came and stood on my fingertips. It tickled a little, but I kept steady and she danced up my arm until she was on my shoulder. Then she whispered in my ear, 'Thank you, Celia.'"

CHAPTER NINE

*E*ven though Celia said she couldn't play, Paul wasn't about to let it go. If she wouldn't come to his house, he would go to hers. He rushed out the back door, yelling, "Ma, I'm going to play at Celia's," and then took off running. He knew if he paused his mother would have stopped him with some chore. Having him take the dog for a walk was her latest thing. The vet had said Clem was overweight and slept too much, but Paul didn't think that was his problem.

When he reached Celia's house, he bounded up the porch steps, a walkie-talkie in each hand. Paul was counting on Celia's Grammy to invite him inside. Once that happened, he'd be the guest and get to decide what they'd play that day. It would be spy games, of course; that was his newest interest. And they'd play in the woods. The weather was warm and pleasant. Way too nice to be stuck indoors.

Paul peered through the screen door into the entryway. Nervously he bounced up and down on the balls of his feet. They'd have to let him in! He'd shifted the walkie-talkies under one arm and was just lifting his hand to knock when he heard voices coming from the living room: first Celia, then an older woman. The words were garbled. Paul turned his head to one side and listened intently but couldn't understand what they were saying. By the sound of Celia's voice, though, they were talking about something really interesting.

A change of plan was in order. Spies had to be adaptable. Slowly he crept back down the steps and sneaked around to the side of the house, where to his relief, the living room windows were open. Crouching down, he pressed his back against the house so he wouldn't be visible. The brick against his spine was uncomfortable, but he took it like a tough guy. A secret agent never complained.

The conversation came out above his head, like sitting below a radio. He held his breath as he heard Celia's grandmother say something about fairies hovering around her, giving off a bright light. She said she'd promised not to tell. He let out a sigh in disappointment. Celia's grandmother was just telling fairy tales. How babyish. Even his own grandmother had enough sense not to treat him like a little kid. Disappointed, he sat down and pulled at a blade of grass until it snapped off.

Celia sounded interested in this fairy stuff, asking her grandmother if she'd been afraid. And her Grammy answered yes, she had been afraid, as if this fairy thing had really happened. Like it was true.

Girls were so weird.

Paul regretted leaving his mini-recorder at home. He'd have loved to have taped this whole discussion so he could listen to it later. If nothing else, it would be fun to play it back to Celia and tease her about it.

His ears perked up when he heard Grammy say, "We probably should keep this story between ourselves. I don't think your parents would appreciate me telling you all this. I know they don't believe me when I say it's true."

"So I can't tell anyone?" Celia asked.

"No, I think this should be our little secret." Grammy's voice floated through the window screen. "I'll tell you the rest of the story later, but for now I'm thinking I should put the chicken and rice in the oven so it's ready when your parents get home. Is this usually when you start your homework?"

"I do it after dinner," Celia said. "Can't we just keep talking about Mira and the rest of them? You said there's so much more."

Her grandmother laughed. "I don't want to use up the whole story all in one afternoon. Don't you think it will be more fun to leave the rest until tomorrow after school?" Paul heard Celia reluctantly agree and then the sound of footsteps as the two left the room. As he crept around the side of the house to make his way home, a thought flew into his head: *Come back tomorrow and bring the recorder.*

Celia would be sorry she'd ditched him.

CHAPTER TEN

*T*hat night, Celia had trouble falling asleep. She shifted from side to back and returned to her side again. Next she rearranged her pillow and tried counting sheep. Finally, after hearing her parents walk past her doorway on the way to their own bedroom, she resorted to the old trick of listening to herself breathe, while imagining her legs getting heavier and heavier. This usually worked.

Just as she felt herself slipping into sleep, she heard a girl's voice call her name. *Celia.* It came from outside. *Celia.* A voice carried on the wind, from the direction of the woods. *Oh, Celia...*

She got out of bed and looked out the french doors that led to the balcony. Complete darkness until—there it was—a flash of light! This time she knew she hadn't imagined it. She opened the door and stepped outside onto the clammy wood of the balcony. The sky was so big, black, and menacing that she hesitated for a moment, but then pushed through her fear and edged over to the railing. Again she heard the voice. It came from the woods, just as she'd thought. *Celia.*

"Yes, I'm here," Celia called out. "Who's there?"

The voice was now inside her head and all around her at the same time. "Celia, we need your help." In an instant, a spot of light darted from the woods and appeared in front of her. A fairy girl, a dazzling beauty with luminous wings and a dress trimmed in ruby colored jewels, fluttered inches from her face.

"Mira," Celia said, with complete certainty. "You're Mira."

The fairy girl nodded. "Listen, Celia, we need your help. This is important."

"Help with what?"

"Vicky McClutchy must be dealt with, do you hear me? She's up to some evil, and you're the only one who can stop her, Celia."

"Vicky McClutchy?" What did this mean? Vicky McClutchy was the woman who wanted to buy her parents' toy company. Celia had seen a photo of her once in a magazine. Vicky was tall and skinny with dark brown hair and a big toothy smile. Not scary at all. Her father didn't like Ms. McClutchy much, and her mother called her ruthless, but she'd never heard them say she was evil.

Mira landed on the railing next to Celia's hand. "Yes, Vicky McClutchy. She must be stopped at any cost. It's up to you, Celia."

"But what…I mean…how am I supposed to stop her? I don't understand."

The fairy girl looked back at the woods in alarm. "I can't stay. It's not safe. Just remember what I told you. Come out to the Triple Trees during the day. Bring the flute, and I'll explain then." She lifted off and called out, "Don't forget."

Celia saw Mira's light get smaller as she traveled farther away. She still had her in her sights when she heard Mira scream, a horrible, painful scream. Celia watched, horrified, as the spot of light disappeared like a candle snuffed out.

"Mira," Celia yelled, her arms reaching out. "What happened, Mira? Come back." The night wrapped itself around her, making it hard for her to breathe. The dark was so intense it blinded her. She gripped the railing, but it dissolved in her hands. "Mira," she screamed. The air got thicker, and she had trouble catching her breath. As she gasped, something pulled her out of her panic.

Cool hands were shaking her. "Celia, wake up. You're dreaming." It was her mother. Celia sat up and gulped air, and then she threw her arms around her mother. Mom stroked her hair and whispered, "Shhh, shh, it was just a dream. You're fine, you're just fine."

"I was dreaming?" Celia said, wiping her eyes.

"Yes," her mother murmured, "it was just a bad dream. You're safe here in your own bed. Dad and I are right down the hall, and the house is locked up tight. Don't worry. Nothing bad can happen anymore. You're safe now."

But it didn't feel like a dream.

CHAPTER ELEVEN

*A*fter Celia fell back asleep, her mother walked down the hall and climbed back into bed.

"Is she okay?" asked her father.

Celia's mother thought carefully before answering. "I'm not sure, really. She's asleep now, but it took a long time for her to calm down. I told her it was just a bad dream, but she insisted it felt real. She kept saying over and over again that Mira told her Vicky McClutchy must be stopped."

"Mira?" Her father sat up. "Are you sure she said the name Mira?"

"Well, yes. I'm sure. Mira told her Vicky McClutchy must be stopped. That's exactly what she said."

"That's so odd." He rubbed his chin. "My mother talked about a Mira when I was about Celia's age. I was having the strangest dreams, and I think my mom was trying to make me feel better. You know I got the idea for *Trixie-Dixie* in a dream when I was just a boy?"

Celia's mother sighed. She'd heard this story at least a hundred times.

"I dreamt about these twin fairy girls who were good deed experts. In my dream, they gave me all the details for the game. I got up the next morning and wrote it all down, and that was the start of *Trixie-Dixie: The Good Deed Game*."

"I heard about the dream before," her mother said, not mentioning that it had been at least a hundred times. "But you never said anything about fairies. I would have remembered that."

Dad cleared his throat. "I always leave out that part, ever since I told Vicky McClutchy about it in fourth grade. She blabbed about it to the whole school, and for the rest of the year I had to listen to 'Jonathan Lovejoy talks to fairies.' You can imagine how mortifying that was."

"Yes, I can imagine that must have been hard."

"I was the laughingstock of the whole school. Even the first graders talked about it. They flapped their arms whenever I walked by. I kept hoping they'd forget, but it lasted all year."

"How terrible," Celia's mother said sympathetically, pulling the blanket up to her chin.

"Terrible doesn't even begin to describe it," Dad grumped, and then he settled back down between the covers. "It was torture. And then there was that business at the National Science Fair in sixth grade. My project was ahead all the way through, but at the last minute she mysteriously got extra points and won first prize. By all rights, that trophy was mine. Have I ever mentioned how much I hate Vicky McClutchy?"

"Only a few thousand times."

They lay silently facing the ceiling. Then Celia's mother said, "Funny that Celia's dream had both Vicky McClutchy and Mira, don't you think?"

Dad sighed. "Probably got the name Mira from talking to her grandmother. And maybe she heard us talking about our business meeting with Vicky." They both thought about their trip to McClutchy Toys—the sleek, thirty-two–story skyscraper with its cold, marble floors and bright lights. Vicky's office was at the top, and was notable for its lack of toys. "What kind of toy company president doesn't have toys in the office?" Celia's father had asked on the drive home.

The offices at Lovejoy World were filled with toys. When Celia came during vacation breaks, there were any number of things to occupy her time. Puzzles and games and stuffed animals sat on shelves and desks and on the floor. Models of pterodactyls and eagles hung from the ceiling. Celia's father was always working on something new, and he welcomed ideas from his employees. The boy who pushed the broom and emptied the trash helped develop a model-sized circus with a trapeze act that worked with pulleys. Marge, the woman in charge of the plush department, brought in new animal ideas from printouts she found on the *National Geographic* Web site.

Happy music played in the office and throughout the factory. Celia's father was a big believer that music affected mood and productivity. Sometimes the workers left their posts to dance. No one minded; in fact, it was expected.

At McClutchy Toys, it was a different story. The offices were as sterile and unwelcoming as an orthodontist's examining room. Their products were manufactured in some other country, so there was no on-site factory.

When Celia's parents had arrived for their business meeting with Vicky McClutchy, her assistant met them with a frown and a raised finger, to indicate he was busy with a phone call. His nameplate said his name was Chase Downe. When Mr. Downe was done reciting a string of numbers, he hung up the phone and asked their names. "Oh yes," he replied. "You are expected." Chase gave the impression he didn't want to be there, which Celia's father thought was too bad because he believed people should like their jobs.

The assistant ushered them into Ms. McClutchy's office, a harshly lit space with a desk large enough for three people. Vicky McClutchy stood looking out the window, her back to the room.

After a minute, Dad cleared his throat to get her attention.

Vicky McClutchy turned around and smiled, showing all her teeth, then crossed the room to meet them. "Jonathan, how good to see you again. And your lovely wife Michelle." She reached out to shake hands. "I think you'll find this meeting to be of great interest. I have an offer you won't be able to refuse."

CHAPTER TWELVE

ornings were so rushed at the Lovejoy residence that Celia didn't get to tell her grandmother about the dream that didn't feel like a dream until she got home from school.

Sitting at the kitchen table, eating tangerine slices (her mother's idea—a nutritious after-school snack), Celia told the whole story in a rush of words. Grammy listened and nodded in recognition when she heard the description of Mira: the way she glowed from within, the lilt of her little voice, and her luminescent wings. When Celia paused, her grandmother said, "So it's begun for you now, too." She sighed. "I wanted you to know about the magic, but I wasn't wishing it would come like this. It doesn't sound like you're off to a good start."

Celia picked up a napkin and wiped at a dribble of juice on her chin. "It was kind of scary, and I'm not sure what I'm supposed to do. Mira's scream was so horrible; it was like she was being attacked. Do you think something bad happened to her?"

Grammy shook her head. "No, I think Mira is fine. The dreams are messages, and sometimes they come out scary when something is very serious. But it might not be as serious as she made it sound. Mira can be a bit of a drama queen sometimes."

"Is it the same Mira you knew, do you think? She looked so young."

Grammy said, "Fairies live far longer than humans. Hundreds of years, I think. Mira would still be quite young, so yes, she is probably the same Mira I knew."

Celia thought for a moment. "But how am I supposed to know what to do?" The enormity of the situation gave her a stomachache. Her biggest problems had always involved math equations and vocabulary words. Stopping evil in its tracks seemed an unreasonable request for a girl her age. "Mira said I should bring the flute and meet her under the Triple Trees. I know what the Triple Trees are. It's a spot out in the woods where Paul and I play all the time, but I don't have a flute. I don't know what she means."

"She said to bring a flute?" Her grandmother tapped her fingers on the tabletop thoughtfully. "A flute? Are you sure?"

"That's what she said. I remember." Like a movie playing in her head, Celia could recall Mira saying those exact words. She knew she'd remember it forever, even if she lived to be as old as her grandmother.

"I know what she's talking about," Grammy said. "The flute was mine when I was a child, and I hid it in my room way back when. We can go up to your room when you're done with your snack and I'll show you where it is."

Celia's room was a bit of a mess, but she was quite sure there wasn't a flute anywhere about. Her mother made her clean every Saturday, and in the spring they emptied her closets and drawers and vacuumed under furniture, even her dresser, which was heavy and required two of them to shove it aside. If there'd been a flute, she'd have known. Clearly her grandmother was confused. "I don't think it can be in my room, Grammy," she said. "I've never seen it."

"It's there all right," her grandmother said. "You've been sleeping over it for years. Finish up your tangerine, and then I'll show you where it is."

A few minutes later, Grammy and Celia pushed her bed away from the wall and pulled the area rug up off the hardwood floor. The section beneath the bed looked the same as in the rest of the room. "It's under one of these," her grandmother said, pointing. "I noticed the board was loose when I was about your age. I hid the flute underneath it so my sister Josie wouldn't get to it. It worked well. No one has ever found my hiding spot."

Celia had never noticed a loose board, and if her parents had, they'd never mentioned it. "Which one is it?" she asked, looking down. Grammy wasn't sure, so Celia crouched down and tried one board after another. All of them were shut tight. "Should I get a screwdriver and start prying them open?" Celia asked.

Her grandmother's forehead furrowed in thought. "Wait just a minute. Let me think." She walked to the center of the room and closed her eyes for what seemed like a long time. Just when Celia was about to ask if she was okay, Grammy's eyes flicked open and she spoke. "Josie's bed was over there." She pointed. "And mine was there on the other side." Her arm moved to the left. "There were two dressers on the wall behind me. And the loose board was—" She hesitated and then slowly her arm swung to one side and aimed itself at Celia's desk. "Right there."

"Are you sure?"

Grammy nodded. "I remember now."

The desk was on rolling casters so it wouldn't scratch the wood. Celia's mother was particular about the hardwood floors. Celia slid the desk smoothly to one side and looked at the floor below.

"That one, right there," her grandmother said, her outstretched arm shaking with anticipation.

As Celia knelt down, her left knee pressed against the wood, causing the plank to pop up. She smiled up at Grammy. "I think we've found it."

Grammy pulled the desk chair forward and sat, leaning forward. "Oh hurry," she said, "I can't wait to see it again after all this time."

The board lifted with a squeak. Below it, Celia found a small metal box. After she took it out, the wood plank dropped with a thud. "It's a little dusty, Grammy," she said, gingerly tapping the top.

"I wouldn't be surprised, after all these years."

Celia blew the dust off the lid, flipped the latch, and opened it. Inside was a leather pouch with a drawstring top. Celia held it in the palm of her hand for a moment, surprised at how light it was.

"Open it, darling. Don't be afraid."

"I'm not afraid. I just thought it would be bigger." Celia tugged at the drawstring and pulled out a silver flute about four inches in length. The first thing she noticed was how it sparkled in the light. The second thing she noticed was that it was broken. "It looks like it's been snapped in two," Celia said. She opened the drawstring bag and looked inside. "What happened to the other half?"

"Let me see." Grammy took the flute and inspected it. "Oh dear, you're right, it is broken. That's odd, it wasn't this way when I saw it the last time." She looked up at Celia. "The other part isn't in the bag?"

Celia turned the bag upside down and shook it. "Nope, and it's not in the metal box." She lifted up the wooden plank and inspected the area beneath. "Not here either."

"Puzzling," her grandmother said. "Maybe Mira will know what happened to the other half. I got the flute from the fairies to begin with, you know."

"You did?"

"Yes, it was a gift from Mira's boss, a fairy named Trapeza. She said I was special. Very few humans can see and hear fairies, you know. That means you and I are very special. The flute was given to me as a thank-you for saving Mira's life. It has magic power, or at least it did before it was broken."

"What magic does it have?" Celia asked.

Grammy said, "As I recall, the true owner of the flute, which was me, was entitled to one wish, but there was a catch. The wish could only be used for something important. There were three rules for wishing, too. The first was that I couldn't wish for more wishes." She laughed. "That's the oldest one in the book, I think, but people still try it, I guess."

"What were the other rules?"

"I don't really remember." Her grandmother had a faraway look in her eyes. "I knew at the time, and I was careful to follow them, but it was so long ago." She reached down and patted Celia's shoulder. "Anyway, you can take that piece with you when you go to talk to Mira and explain that's how you found it."

Celia turned the instrument over and inspected it. Her half only had two openings: a bowl-shaped blowhole and one opening below that. She lifted the flute to her lips, but no matter how hard she blew, no sound came out. She looked at her grandmother with disappointment. "It doesn't work anymore."

"Back when I had it, it only worked when you really needed it." Grammy stroked Celia's hair and tucked a loose strand behind her ear. "I only blew into it once, and that was right before I made my wish. It made the most beautiful music. That's how I knew my wish would come true."

"And what was your wish?"

"It's very complicated," her grandmother said. "Someday, when you're a little older, I'll tell you the whole story."

"I really don't understand any of this," Celia said with a sad shake of her head.

"You don't need to be worried, darling. Mira will explain what you'll need to know. Go on out to the woods and talk to her. It will all work out. You'll see."

"Will you go with me?" Celia felt a surge of doubt mixed with fear. The frightening dream was still on her mind. But nothing bad could happen if her grandmother was with her, she was sure of it.

"Oh no, darling. I can't see or hear fairies anymore." Grammy shook her head sadly. "My time for magic is long past. This is something you have to do for yourself."

CHAPTER THIRTEEN

*T*he path into the woods had been there as long as Celia could remember. Oddly enough, it never became overgrown with weeds, even though it rarely got much foot traffic. Her father said it had been there when he was a boy as well and that the grass had been stamped down for so many years that it always remembered to lie flat.

Celia headed down the path with the flute in hand. It would take a few minutes to get to the place she and Paul called the Triple Trees, three trees clustered so close together that their highest branches interlaced like they were holding hands. The space beneath the trees was shady, even on the brightest days. The Triple Trees felt like magic to Celia, and when she and Paul played there, their pretend games always took on an otherworldly sensation.

She walked slowly, mindful of the chirping of birds and the way the breeze whipped the grass on either side of her. Celia was aware of everything around her, it seemed, except that she was being followed.

CHAPTER FOURTEEN

*W*hen Grammy answered the knock at the front door, she was surprised to see Vicky McClutchy standing there. "Why if it isn't little Vicky all grown up," she said with a grin. "I haven't seen you in more years than I can count. You look wonderful."

Vicky flashed a wide smile, her lips stretching over a row of brilliant white teeth. "Hi, Mrs. Lovejoy, it's good to see you too."

"I'm sorry, dear, but I'm the only one here. My son and his wife are at work, and Celia is out right now. If you want to try Jonathan at his office, I can give you the number."

"Oh no." Vicky McClutchy held up a hand. "I came to see you, actually. I was hoping we could have a little talk."

"Well, of course. Come on in." Once they were settled at the kitchen table with cinnamon tea and butter cookies, Grammy said, "I read in the paper that you're now involved in the county government. How do you find time to run a company and serve on the county board?"

"Not too many people could manage so well," Vicky said, sipping her tea, "but the county really needed someone strong to take charge, so I make time. We have a lot of new projects in the works, particularly in the transportation department. This county has been in need of an updated highway system for eons. I think people will be very surprised at some of our plans."

"I had no idea," Grammy said. "Good for you. And I see your sister has been taking good care of your parents' old house." For over a hundred years, the Lovejoys and the McClutchys had been neighbors. Celia's grandmother was old enough to remember Vicky's grandfather when he was a little boy, and all the children and grandchildren that came after that.

"Yes, my sister and her husband got the house after my folks retired to Florida." Vicky broke a cookie in half and sighed. "I wanted it, which would have only been fair since I am older, but they thought it should go to her since it was a family home and she has a child." She made a face.

"Ah, yes, your nephew, Paul. He and Celia are good friends, I understand. Such a nice boy."

Vicky waved a hand in the air. "Yes, that's the one. Paul." She sighed heavily and then took a sip of tea. "Anyway, the reason I wanted to talk to you is because I was hoping you could talk some sense into that son of yours. We had a business meeting and I made him the offer of a lifetime, but he says he's not interested. His wife was willing to listen, but Jonathan walked right out of my office without even letting me finish. People don't walk out on me very often, I can tell you that much." Her eyes narrowed.

Grammy laughed. "I'm not sure I can help you with that. Jonathan has always been rather strong-minded. Even as a child, he was stubborn."

"I remember," Vicky said. "There was a time when we were best friends. We did everything together. And then one day he wouldn't play with me anymore. I came to the door and he just sent me away, said he didn't want to come out. And that was it. The end of everything."

"Children do outgrow friendships, I guess." Grammy gave her a sympathetic look. "That's the sad truth of it."

Vicky shook her head. "But we were *best* friends. We did everything together." She vividly recalled the hurt and shock of that day. After Jonathan had shut the door in her face, she'd walked home crying. Then she'd locked herself in her bedroom and tore the head off every doll she owned. The anger had stuck with her all these years. It was Jonathan's fault she never was happy again. He had to make a big deal out of the fact that she'd told the other kids his secret about the fairy dream. So what if she did? That wasn't a good reason to end a friendship. He'd overreacted. Vicky swallowed and continued. "Best friends for years, and then—nothing. I haven't had a best friend since. Not that I need a best friend," she added hurriedly. "I'm a serious businesswoman. If you want to build a multimillion-dollar company, you can't afford to spend time socializing. Friends are for people who have nothing better to do."

"I heard that you were very successful," Grammy said. "Good for you. Your hard work paid off." She reached for the teapot and added to their cups. "So what did you want with Jonathan then? I can't imagine he has much to offer someone like you. He's just a small business owner. He and Michelle work more for the love of it than the money. They aren't getting rich, that's for sure."

Vicky tapped her hand against the table, making the cups rattle. "That's why it's so infuriating that he won't listen to my offer. He doesn't have to work so hard for so little. I'm willing to pay him more than he would make in a lifetime if he'd sell me his business. He and Michelle could do anything with the kind of money I'm talking about. They could retire for life."

Grammy looked surprised. "The business? But dear, Jonathan wouldn't ever sell Lovejoy World. It's his life, his calling. He adores making toys and games that make children happy. The work they do there makes the world a better place."

"Oh please." Vicky puffed up her cheeks and blew air out, exasperated. "It's just a company, Mrs. Lovejoy. Profit and loss statements. Employee paychecks. Hiring and firing people and keeping your eye on them to make sure they don't steal from you. Suppliers and vendors, blah, blah, blah." She waved a hand in the air. "The world is what it is. If Jonathan thinks his toys and games are making a difference, he's fooling himself."

"If running a business is so much trouble, why would you want to buy Jonathan's?" Grammy asked.

Vicky smiled and stirred her tea. "For the challenge. With my business sense, I think I could turn Lovejoy World around and make it a big moneymaker. "

Grammy gave Vicky a puzzled look. "And how would you do that?"

"Once I bought it, I'd own the rights to all the games and toys, of course. With some changes, a few of them could be the hot toys of next season. The rest I'd eliminate. To further cut costs, I'd have everything manufactured overseas."

"But what about the employees?" Grammy asked.

"The Lovejoy employees would get the opportunity to find other jobs elsewhere."

"You'd fire the employees?" Grammy was aghast, thinking about all the people who worked at Lovejoy World: J.J., the boy who pushed the broom; Manuel, the electronics wizard; Marge, who designed the stuffed animals; and all the ladies who chatted as they assembled the toys and brought cookies as treats for the others. She'd visited her son's business many times and was always impressed by the care and pride put into the work. What would the employees do if they came to the factory one day and were locked out? This wasn't just a job for them. It was their life. "You can't fire the employees! They're like family."

Vicky shrugged. "It happens all the time in business. You can't get too sentimental if you want to run a successful company. I've learned to cut out the dead weight. I wouldn't worry about the employees. If they have half a brain, they'll find other jobs. If they can't, it's their own fault."

"Well," Grammy said, "I must say that I'm very glad Jonathan is not taking your offer."

Vicky shrugged. "Just because he hasn't taken my offer yet doesn't mean this is over. I don't give up that easily."

Grammy smiled. "Yes, I think I remember how determined you were even as a child. You won the National Science Fair award one year, didn't you?"

"Yes, first place. Jonathan was second." Vicky smiled at the memory. She still had the trophy in her condo downtown. Sometimes she took it off the shelf and polished it. She loved to remember the look on Jonathan's face when they called her name as the winner. He'd been so sure he had won, but she'd been victorious instead. Now she found it infuriating that Jonathan's toys won all the awards while hers were passed over by the judges because they were too violent.

Grammy stirred her tea. "I wish you luck, my dear, but if I were you, I wouldn't count on Jonathan changing his mind. His company is everything to him. He wouldn't sell it for all the tea in China."

Vicky grinned. Foolish old lady. Clearly she didn't realize it was a mistake to underestimate Vicky McClutchy.

CHAPTER FIFTEEN

*C*elia walked into the center of the Triple Trees, protected by the canopy of branches overhead. She thought about all the times she'd come here with Paul. This spot had always felt special, but was it magic?

With fumbling fingers she loosened the drawstring on the bag, then pulled out the flute. Even in the shade, the silver glistened. She'd never seen metal like this before—it glittered like diamonds. To think that something so magical and lovely had been in her room all those years, right under her feet, and she'd never known.

Something scampered through the underbrush, startling her, but she didn't see anything. A bunny or squirrel maybe? She held her breath and listened again, but whatever it was had gone.

Now she was alone in the woods, about to call a fairy girl with a magic flute. Her heart began to pound the same way it did when she ventured out in the dark, and she knew it was now or never. Celia lifted the flute to her lips and blew softly into the hole. No sound came out, but the space around her became charged with electricity and she saw a bright ball of light in the distance coming her way.

She lowered the hand holding the flute to her side and took a deep breath. Fairies were real then! She'd believed her grandmother, or at least she had *wanted* to believe her grandmother, but one small part of her had wondered if her parents were right, that all the fairy talk was nonsense. Her mother and father usually knew everything. But not this time.

The light pulsed closer to Celia, zipping through the air in a zigzag pattern. The fairy stopped a foot from Celia's face, her wings fluttering fast and furious, like a hummingbird hovering in midair.

The Triple Trees leaned forward slightly in admiration, and Celia caught a whiff of honey and cinnamon. The fairy girl in front of her matched the image she'd seen in her dream, but she had to be sure. "Mira?" she asked, once she found her voice.

"Of course. Who else?" Mira smoothed the front of her frock as she bobbed in place. She was resplendent in a glittery silver dress, as shiny bright as the flute. Her voice had a saucy tone Celia hadn't been expecting. Her grandmother had made fairies sound like they were all goodness and light, but Mira had the kind of edge to her voice that Paul's mother called "smart," as in "There's no need to get smart about it, mister."

A small crowd of fairies gathered nearby in a midair cluster. Celia was afraid to take her eyes off Mira, but at a glance she saw there were about a dozen of them, boys and girls, and all dazzlingly beautiful. They wore glimmering clothing in various shades and were as unique as snowflakes—no two had the same skin tone or hair color. Their wings moved quickly in an iridescent blur.

Seeing Celia's look, Mira said, "Don't pay any attention to them. They haven't seen a real person up close like I have, so they'll be gawking." She turned and motioned for them to scoot, and they flew back a few feet. "Bunch of fledglings. I tried to leave them behind, but there was no stopping them once they learned we'd be meeting."

"I got your message in my dream," Celia said shyly. "My grandmother helped me find where she hid the flute."

"Your grandmother?" Mira tapped her fingers together, thinking. "Oh yes, the original Celia. The finest human being ever. You look a lot like her. Or at least like she used to look. You humans get older so much faster than we do."

"Have you known a lot of people?" Celia asked. She extended her arm in a graceful curve, and Mira landed on her wrist.

"I've known my share of people. I've been assigned to your house since I reached the rank of fairy master class. I've done a good job of it, if I do say so myself."

Behind her the other fairies twittered with laughter. Mira turned in irritation to scold them. "It's not boasting if it's true. Since I've watched over your house, there's been more joy than sadness, and your family has put light and positivity out into the world. Positivity is our main goal. It's the best you can do," she explained to Celia, hopscotching up her arm. "Evil can't thrive in a positive environment. That's one of our precepts."

"What's a precept?" Celia asked.

"A precept is a saying that sums up what we're about and gives us direction. Our precepts help us remember what we need to do. Our work is very important. Without us, the world would be a horrible, horrible place."

"In my dream you said something about evil. Your scream was so terrible, I thought something awful had happened. I was really worried and scared," Celia said.

Mira said, "I didn't mean to scare you, but I needed to get your attention. It worked."

"So there isn't an emergency?" Celia asked, puzzled.

"Oh, there's an emergency all right." Mira tossed back her hair. "I just don't know the details yet, but I can feel it coming, and it has to do with Vicky McClutchy."

"The one who wants to buy my parents' company?" Celia said.

Mira nodded. "The very same."

"But I know all about that. I heard them talking about it one night." From her perch on the landing, Celia had heard her parents rehash the meeting at McClutchy Toys. Her father had ranted about "that woman" and vowed never to talk to her again. "She wanted to buy Lovejoy World, and my father said no. When he says no, that's it." She knew from firsthand experience how stubborn her father could be. He never budged.

"I'm sorry to have to say this, but you are wrong." Mira waved a finger close to Celia's nose. "Vicky McClutchy is crafty. She's ingenious at getting what she wants. I've seen her do it again and again. Even when she was a little girl she'd stop at nothing to get her way, bending the rules and cheating with no regard for anyone else."

"Can't you put good suggestions in her head?" Celia asked. "That's what my grandmother said fairies do. Just use your magic and make her good."

"Hah!" Mira tapped a foot. "If it were that simple, don't you think we would have thought of that ourselves?" Behind her the group of fairies twittered with laughter. "That's enough," Mira shouted over her shoulder. "It's not her fault. She doesn't know our ways yet."

"I don't understand what you want me to do," Celia said. "I don't have any powers or magic. And the flute is broken." She held it up. "I could only find one half."

"Well, that's a problem," Mira said, flapping a hand. "You need to find the other half pronto. But even without it, you do have power. All humans do, but most of them don't know it. We fairies can only nudge people in the right direction and ward off evil when we can. We're that little voice in your head making suggestions. Guiding you even when you feel like you're all alone. That's all we can do, but sometimes it's enough. Sometimes it's not."

One of the other fairy girls flew closer. "Tell her about Paul," the girl said, zinging around her excitedly.

"I was getting to that," Mira said impatiently.

"What about Paul?" Celia wondered.

"I have the feeling Paul is going to play an important part in helping you on this assignment. He's your connection to Vicky McClutchy." Mira was so close to her face, Celia almost went cross-eyed.

"Vicky McClutchy is Paul's aunt!" said a fairy boy with an impish grin. "She grew up next door!"

"She's his aunt?" Now Celia was really confused. Paul never mentioned having an Aunt Vicky, and her parents only referred to her as the owner of McClutchy Toys. No one had ever linked her to the neighborhood. "Really? But Paul never talks about her."

"She's really his aunt, his mother's sister. And boy, those two girls did not get along when they were growing up," Mira said, flying away from Celia and waving an arm like sword-fighting. "Vicky is one bad cookie. If she were my aunt, I wouldn't talk about her either."

Celia could feel the movement of fairies circling her. One of them landed on her shoulder and grabbed her hair for support. "I'm not sure what you want me to do. My grandmother said you would explain what I need to know."

"Oh yes, your grandmother," Mira said, smiling. "She was such a good friend to the Watchful Woods fairies and me in particular. She saved my life, you know."

"That was when Mira was out at night by herself," another fairy said in a singsong voice. "Precept number two—never go out at night alone. That's when the shadow things lurk in the dark. Everyone knows that."

"Okay, enough about that, Garnet," Mira grumbled. "All fairies makes mistakes when they're just starting out. Besides, it was a long time ago, and I was just a fledgling. Let's get back to the subject at hand, which is Vicky McClutchy. Boyd here," Mira said as she jabbed a thumb in the direction of a smiling boy fairy to her right, "never did have much luck getting through to Vicky in her growing up years, and now she's set in her ways."

"Hey," Boyd protested. "It's not my fault I got a tough case. You got it easy with your assignment. The Lovejoys are naturally good. Anyone could be successful if they had that house."

"Anyway," Mira said to Celia, "for now your assignment is this—find the other half of the flute. Trust me, you're going to need it. Oh, and you also need to keep an eye on things and report back to us when you know more about what's going on with your father and Vicky."

"But there won't be any more to tell," Celia said. "Vicky McClutchy asked to buy my parents' company and my dad said no. It's all over."

"Trust me," Mira said. "It's not over yet."

CHAPTER SIXTEEN

*P*aul waited until Celia left the clearing and was a safe distance away before clicking off the tape recorder. What the heck was she doing out there talking to herself like a crazy person? He tucked the recorder into his pocket for safekeeping.

After he'd followed her out to the Triple Trees, he crouched behind a bush to spy. She'd lifted some kind of whistle to her lips, but he didn't hear a sound. The next part was the most confusing. Celia started talking to no one, asking questions and acting excited and nervous. At one point it looked like she was calling her arm "Mira." And then, weirdest of all, she kept saying his name and his aunt's name. What the heck was that all about?

Girls liked to make stuff up, Paul knew that. When they were younger, Celia was always trying to get him to play school or pioneer days or some other lame thing. But he'd never seen anything like this before. Why would she pretend by herself? Maybe it would make sense once he listened to the recording at home.

He dawdled down the path toward his house and was lost in thought when a hand grabbed the back of his shirt, making him yelp in surprise. "Aunt Vicky," he stammered. "What are you doing here?"

"I might ask the same thing of you, you little runt." She smiled, but it wasn't a happy look. "This is the Lovejoy's private property. You're trespassing."

"I know it's their property," he said, gulping. She still had a tight hold on his collar. With a little more force, she'd lift him right off his feet. "It's okay if I play here. Celia and I do it all the time."

"Nice story, but I just saw the girl go by a few minutes ago and she looked very unhappy. What did you do to her?" Aunt Vicky released her grip and put her face up to his. Her eyes narrowed accusingly.

"I didn't do anything, I swear," Paul said. "We weren't even playing together. I was spying on her and I recorded her with this." He pulled it out to show her. "Celia was all by herself in the woods and was talking to no one. She kept going on and on about magic and fairies and stuff. She kept saying your name, too."

"Really. Fairies, you say? And she was talking about me? Why am I not surprised?" Aunt Vicky snorted. "The whole family is loony. Like father, like daughter, I guess." She forced the recorder out of his hands. "I'll take this, thank you." She turned and strode away toward his house.

"But you'll give it back, right, Aunty Vicky?" Paul called as he tried to catch up. "Cause I really need it. It's part of my spy kit. Okay?"

"Don't worry, kid, you'll get it back." Vicky didn't slow down and didn't turn around. Paul's mom always said Aunt

Vicky never gave anyone an inch. Paul rushed to stay along-side her. She said, "I'm staying at your house all week while my condo gets painted."

This was news. Paul knew about Aunt Vicky's million-dollar condo in the city because his mother had shown him photos of it in a magazine. He and his parents had never been invited to visit, but he didn't care. It didn't look like his type of place anyway. Lots of oddball sculptures and ex-pensive furniture. Nothing fun at all. "Does my mom know you're staying with us? She never said you're gonna be stay-ing at our house this week." His aunt kept walking, a deter-mined look on her face. "Aunt Vicky?"

His aunt waved away his concerns. "She'll find out when I tell her."

CHAPTER SEVENTEEN

When Celia saw Paul coming her way in the school cafeteria, she wanted to hide under the table. He wore an oversized hoodie, slouchy pants, and a goofy grin that widened as he got closer. She chewed her ham and cheese sandwich and looked down, hoping he wouldn't stop to talk.

"Hey, Celia," he said, a little too loudly.

She swallowed before answering. "Hey." The other girls at the table stopped what they were doing to look. Mentally she wished Paul away. *Not now! Not here! Go back to your own spot, Paul!* It was one thing to talk on the bus or after school. Nobody really noticed, and if anyone commented, she could easily explain. *I have to be nice to him—he's my neighbor.* But here in the cafeteria, in front of the whole school? That was another story. Talk about awkward.

Oblivious to the stares, Paul bobbed his head and said, "Hey, Celia, I was thinking maybe you could come over and help finish that castle after school. It's gonna be really cool when it's all done."

"I don't think so," Celia said. Next to her, Sasha Turner snickered.

"But you hafta come." He looked let down. "Last week you said you could come over next week, and now this week *is* the next week. You said you would. You promised!"

Celia didn't remember promising, though it was possible. She'd given him the brush-off on the bus but couldn't recall the exact wording. "Paul, I told you my grandmother needs me to be with her after school." She lowered her voice. "I'm not coming over to your house anymore." Her cheeks flushed red with embarrassment.

"Go away, little boy," called out a girl on the far end of the table. Her name was Bethany or Bethanne or something like that. A sixth grader.

Celia stared down at her plastic bag full of carrot sticks. Beneath the table, Paul's shoes were within view, and they weren't moving.

"My aunt Vicky is staying with us this week. She owns this cool company, McClutchy Toys, and she brought a new game system and all these cool games, even the kind I'm not allowed to play. You gotta come. It's boring playing all by myself."

Celia's head jerked up at the mention of his aunt's name. "Your aunt Vicky? Why is she staying with you?"

"She's at our house until her condo is done getting painted. All week probably. My mom says it's gonna be one long week." Paul drummed his fingers on the table. "The games she brought are really cool. Really cool! Please, Celia? Will you come?"

"Maybe," Celia said quietly. "I have to check with my Grammy first to see if it's okay."

"And if she says yes, then you'll come over?" His face lit up.

Celia leaned over and whispered, "Yes, then I'll come over. You better go now, Paul. We can talk on the bus."

CHAPTER EIGHTEEN

*C*elia asked for permission to play at Paul's after school, and her grandmother thought it was a good idea. "This will give you a chance to see what Vicky McClutchy is up to," Grammy said thoughtfully. "If the fairies are right, she's got something up her sleeve."

"Mira said she's a bad cookie," Celia said.

"No one is all bad or all good," her grandmother said. "Everyone has their reasons for the way they act. In this case, Vicky McClutchy isn't bad, she's just misguided. She can only see things from her point of view, so she doesn't understand how her actions affect other people. It's a very sad way to be."

"When I'm at Paul's, should I look through her things and spy on her?" Celia asked.

"Oh bless you, no." Her grandmother smoothed Celia's hair. "Vicky will probably be at work this time of day. Just spend time with Paul and keep your eyes and ears open. Things happen when they're supposed to happen."

When Celia arrived at Paul's house, he was waiting at the front door. "Yay, Celia, you're here! I hoped and hoped you'd come."

In the foyer, Celia was greeted by the smell of frying onions. She hung her coat on the peg behind the door and followed Paul to the den. He was in a chatty mood and didn't stop talking, not once, not even when his mother called from the kitchen for them not to make a mess and to please keep the volume down. Celia said a silent thank-you that she no longer had to come here after school.

Paul and Celia settled down in front of the large TV. Next to it, the dog, Clem, snored loudly in his usual spot. Paul chose a game that involved following ordinary people who randomly turned into something scary—a monster, a vampire, a zombie—there were a dozen possibilities in all. You never knew what the people would turn into, or when— this was the worst part for Celia, who hated being both surprised and scared. Each evil creature required a different method of killing. If you got it wrong, they killed you, and it wasn't a pretty sight. Blood and guts everywhere.

Celia knew her parents wouldn't approve. "How come your mom is letting you play this?" she asked, after being mutilated for the eleventh time.

"It's just while Aunt Vicky is here." Paul kept his eyes on the screen and chewed his lower lip in concentration. "She's paying us a lot of money to try it out and tell her what I like about it and what I don't. My dad is taking most of it for my college money, but I get to keep some of it."

"Like how much money?" Celia asked, putting her controller down. She'd had enough.

"One thousand dollars!" Paul said, his eyes widening. "And I get to have fifty of it all for me. Woo hoo!"

Celia mulled this over. It was an outrageous amount of money just for playing a game. "Do you like your Aunt Vicky?"

Paul didn't answer, just shrugged his shoulders.

"Is she nice to you?"

"She's okay, I guess," he said. "My mom says that Aunt Vicky just isn't a kid person."

Celia sat and watched Paul play. She'd never seen him sit so quietly. Usually energy shot off him. He'd hop from foot to foot or drum his fingers. Even when sitting, he usually fidgeted. Not now. This game had some kind of hold on him. It was impossible to hold a conversation when his eyes were like this—glazed and unblinking. Getting information about his aunt today didn't seem likely.

Just when Celia was thinking of going home, the door to the den burst open, making her jump. Vicky McClutchy stood in the doorway. Celia recognized her from a magazine picture but hadn't known she was so tall. Vicky was a slender, pretty woman, who dressed like a lady in a catalog—gray pants and a burgundy jacket over a white shirt. Dangly earrings and shiny hair. Nothing like Paul's mother, her sister.

"I want you kids to clear out of here," Vicky said, by way of a greeting. "I need to make a phone call." She held up a cell phone. "I mean it, squirt," she said to Paul, who hadn't budged. "Vamoose. You and your little girlfriend need to leave. I have an important business call."

"She's not my girlfriend." Paul looked up, annoyed. "This is Celia. She lives in the next house over."

"I know who she is," Vicky said, "and I don't really care. Do I have to call your mother and tell her you're not listening?" She looked toward Celia and fingered a silver chain around her neck. Something shimmering and cylindrical hung off the chain. When Vicky pulled it out from behind the flap of her jacket, Celia's mouth dropped open in shock. It was the other half of the flute.

"Can't you call in another room?" Paul whined.

"No, this one has the best reception. Beat it, you two."

Paul reluctantly set down his controller and shut off the game and TV. Celia followed him to his bedroom, where he plunked himself down on the floor. He had the sullen look he got when things didn't go his way. "She always ruins everything," he said. "She even made my mom cry last night."

"She made your mom cry?" Celia had trouble imagining this. "What did she say that made her cry?"

"I'm not exactly sure," Paul admitted. "They made me go to my room after a while. There was talking and yelling, and my mom started crying. Then my dad asked my aunt to leave the house. He was really, really mad. That's when Aunt Vicky said she'd pay me for playing the game, so they talked about it, and she gets to stay for a week."

"Wow," Celia said.

Paul looked down at the floor. "I asked my mom about it. She said it was nothing I should worry about." Both of them were silent for a minute. If a parent said it was nothing to worry about, it was probably serious.

"Sometimes I listen to my mom and dad at night when they think I'm in bed," Celia said. "I find out things that way. You could do that."

"I tried that, but I didn't hear anything. It's about our house, though, I know that much. My mom told my dad that Vicky was mad she didn't get the house, so now she's going to make sure we can't have it either. My dad says my aunt is a bad person."

"She's not bad, just misguided," Celia said, quoting Grammy.

"Nope, she's pretty bad. And selfish, too. She never thinks of anyone but herself." Paul made a face. "She's my worstest relative. I like my dad's sister much, much better."

The two sat quietly for a minute, until Celia asked, "Paul, what do you know about that flute necklace your aunt has?"

"That silver thing?"

She nodded.

"She just always wears it. It's her good luck charm, she says."

"Does she ever take it off?" Celia asked.

"I don't know. I don't think so. No, wait." He rested his chin on the bed. "She puts it on the nightstand when she sleeps. I looked in and saw it yesterday morning when the door was open and she wasn't up yet. How come you want to know?" He pulled out a tissue and blew his nose.

Celia ignored the question and thought. She needed to get that flute back, but in the meantime she had to deal with poor Paul. He was a mess. "It'll be okay, Paul. I'm sure she can't get your house. You already live here, right?"

"I guess." He sniffled. Celia went across the hall to the bathroom and came back with a box of tissues. Paul blew his nose and looked at her gratefully. "Thanks, Celia. You're really the best, best friend ever. I'm sorry I spied on you. Really, really sorry. Please don't be mad."

"You spied on me? What are you talking about?"

"Yesterday in the woods. I followed you and tape-recorded when you were pretending and talking about fairies, and saying my aunt's name and stuff."

Celia felt the blood drain from her face. "Did you see anybody besides me?"

Paul shook his head. "No, just you."

"What else? Did you hear anyone else talking?"

"No, I was pretty far away."

She grabbed his arm. "Did you see the lights?"

"Ouch, Celia, stop it. You're hurting me." Paul pulled his arm away. "No, I didn't see any lights or anything. Just you."

"What did you do with the recording?"

"My aunt played it when we got home," Paul said sheepishly.

"You told your aunt about it?"

Seeing her face, he said, "Don't be mad, Celia. She saw me out in the woods after you left. She made me tell. It's not my fault, really. We listened to it, but we couldn't hear much cause I was so far away. Really, we couldn't! We just heard you say at the end that you didn't know how to stop Vicky McClutchy. That was the only thing that came out clearly."

Celia gulped. "What did your aunt say?"

"She laughed this really creepy laugh and said, 'No one can stop Vicky McClutchy.'"

Oh no, Celia thought. This was serious. Vicky had the other half of the flute, and now she had plans to take over her father's company and Paul's house. Something major needed to be done, and quickly. Before even thinking it through, she blurted out, "Paul, I need your help."

CHAPTER NINETEEN

When the kids left the room, Vicky settled back in the recliner and opened her cell phone. She usually had her assistant make her calls, but this was one she wanted to handle personally. By summertime this old ruin of a place, her childhood home—the house that really should have been hers—would be gone.

She envisioned a wrecking ball swinging through the front window and smiled. She'd make sure her sister and that boring husband of hers had time to move out, of course, long before the new highway construction began. She wasn't that coldhearted. They'd plead and beg, but she wouldn't give in—if anything, they'd already had the house far longer than they deserved. And this was a fair deal. They'd wind up with enough money to go somewhere else and buy a different, better house. Hopefully far enough away that she wouldn't have to see them that often. Especially the boy. If she had to hear that Paul whine one more time, she was going to strangle him.

Vicky wanted to be there when her sister got the official news, so she'd lied about her condo being painted and needing a place to stay. Of course, they believed it. Once she was there, she couldn't resist dropping a hint about the upcoming demolition. The county was considering it, she told them, just wanting to see their reaction. She loved what she saw next.

"They can't do that!" her sister had shouted. "We'll fight it. This is our home."

Her brother-in-law comforted his wife and glared at Vicky through his dorky glasses. "I think you should leave," he'd said. Then they sent the kid to his room, and the whole thing had blown into a big deal. Vicky finally smoothed things over by saying it wasn't for sure yet and she'd help them fight it. As if. Then she offered them a thousand dollars for the boy's college fund. They took it, which was ironic because she doubted Paul would ever be accepted at any college. He didn't seem bright enough.

The main reason behind this whole project had been to destroy Jonathan Lovejoy's house. Bulldozed right to the ground, that was the plan. She smiled. That's what he got for snubbing her and turning down her offer to buy his company. You mess with Vicky McClutchy, you lose big-time. That was the lesson here.

It had been a good day when she was appointed to the county board. The first woman who ever held that position, too. It was only local government and an honorary title, but it was a start. Once she started throwing her money around, she was practically running the place. Making decisions that affected the masses suited her all too well. The public was too stupid to know what was best for them anyway. It didn't take long after she joined the board before she was completely in charge. Having control of the county board made her a powerful woman. Power and money, that's what she wanted, and that's what she had, thanks to her good luck charm.

She fingered the flute necklace and smiled, thinking of the day in fourth grade when she'd stolen it from Jonathan. He himself had stolen it from his mother's secret hiding place, so he wasn't so innocent himself. He'd taken it out from underneath the floorboards in his room, he told her, swearing her to secrecy. She'd promised but kept her fingers crossed behind her back. After she'd left his house with the flute in her pocket, he'd figured out that she had it and came after her. He found her in the woods, looking for the fairies he always talked about.

"Give it back," he'd said, rushing at her. "It won't work for you anyway."

He'd grabbed hold of her arm, pressing so hard it left finger marks. They'd struggled, but she held tight to the flute. He finally got a grip on it and tried to twist it out of her hand. That was when it snapped in half. Surprising, really, that such hard metal broke so easily. Jonathan fell back onto the ground and stared in shock at his half, which gave her a chance to run home. She heard him calling behind her. "It's not yours," he yelled, and she thought, *It is now.* She was going to give it back when he called and apologized, but he never did. She guessed he was probably still mad she'd told everyone at school he'd dreamt about fairies, as if that was any big deal. In any case, the friendship was over.

Once in high school she went up to him in the hall and showed him the flute, which now hung around her neck on a chain. "Remember this?" she'd said. He gave her a blank look and claimed not to know what she was talking about.

She was the one who had the last laugh, though. He said it wouldn't work for her, and yet it did. Wasn't she the richest, most powerful woman in the county? Maybe in the state. And it would only get better. There was no way she could have accomplished all this on her own. Even if she only had half the flute, she must have the magic part, since Jonathan hadn't amounted to much by comparison. Yes, she had the better half.

Vicky punched the numbers into the phone. "It's me," she said when the call went through to the county office. "Vicky McClutchy. Put the paperwork through and let's get this show on the road. The sooner we get these houses demolished, the sooner we can start."

Jonathan Lovejoy and her sister would be sorry they'd ever messed with her.

CHAPTER TWENTY

*D*eep in the woods, Mira stopped mid-flight and cocked her head to one side. "Shh," she said to Jasmine, the fledgling who flew alongside her.

"What is it?" Jasmine asked, her wings fluttering fast to hold her in place.

"It's the girl, Celia."

Mira's face was squinched like she was thinking hard, but Jasmine knew that what she was really doing was getting a read on the people in her house. It wasn't enough to watch them, Mira always said; you had to feel their emotions and sense their thoughts. Only then could a fairy give her people guidance. Getting assigned a house and a family was a big responsibility, and it was more complicated than Jasmine had initially thought. She'd been training with Mira for days and still didn't feel nearly ready to take on her own assignment. "What about the girl?"

"She found the other half of the flute and is working on a plan to get it back. If she succeeds, she'll possess some very old and powerful magic," Mira said. "Almost too powerful for one little girl. I hope she uses it wisely."

"Can't you help her? Maybe get the flute for her?"

Mira sighed. "You know that's not how it works. We can't get directly involved."

"But we already got directly involved, didn't we?" Jasmine asked, her head tipped to one side. "Because the flute came from us in the first place."

Mira said, "You're right, but it didn't come from me. It was our boss, Trapeza, who gave the original Celia the magic flute after she saved my life. Trapeza told me the flute would only work for Celia or someone in her family. Otherwise, it's just a piece of metal. Very shiny, pretty metal, but not magical at all. The magic in the flute has been passed down to young Celia, so she has to be the one to get it back."

"So this little girl has to do everything herself? That doesn't seem fair. What if she can't?" Jasmine said.

"As I told you before," Mira said impatiently, "it's our job to encourage and guide, not to take over. This new Celia will have to figure it out on her own. It's the only way. You know, doing the right thing is never easy, but it's always right," Mira said. "Are you getting all this, Jasmine? You'll be taking over your new assignment very soon. It's important to know all this. I'm not talking just to flap my lips."

"I'm paying attention, really I am, Mira. I want to do the best job I can for the family. I'll make you proud, I promise."

Secretly Mira doubted Jasmine was ready to take on her own family, especially the challenging one she was being given, but it wasn't up to her. Mira was only the regional fairy master, and the orders came from her superior. Boyd was being pulled from his assignment, thank goodness, and Jasmine would replace him. Normally fairies served a hundred-year term, but Boyd had failed to live up to his responsibility despite many, many chances. In fact, he had failed completely. There was so much unhappiness in his assigned house, it was a crime. The boy, Paul, was generally miserable; his parents, dull and tired.

Yes, they needed help, and Mira agreed that a fresh new recruit was probably the answer, but Jasmine? She was such a fledgling, it was doubtful she was up to the hard work that needed to be done. Still, Mira knew it wasn't up to her. The orders came from above. All she could do was train Jasmine and hope for the best. "Okay then, listen up. There will be a test later."

CHAPTER TWENTY-ONE

When Celia got home from Paul's, she had just enough time to give her grandmother an update before her parents were due to arrive home from work.

"So Vicky has the other half of the flute? You're sure?" Grammy asked, puzzled. She stood at the stove stirring a pot of beef barley soup.

"I'm sure. It was exactly like mine." The sight of Vicky McClutchy fingering the flute necklace was fresh in her mind. There was no doubt.

"How could she have gotten it?"

"I don't know," Celia said, "but Paul's going to help me get it back. He doesn't like his aunt much at all. He said he'd take the flute off his aunt's nightstand when she's sleeping."

Grammy frowned. "I don't think it's a good idea to get Paul involved."

"I didn't tell him about the fairies and the magic," Celia said hurriedly. "I just said it belonged to our family since my grandmother was a little girl."

"Still, it's not right to ask a friend to take a risk that will get him in trouble." Grammy's stern look made Celia feel small.

"Would you help then? Maybe you could call and ask Paul's aunt to give the flute back?" Celia asked, certain that Vicky would be more likely to listen to a grown-up.

"It doesn't work that way," Grammy said gently. "I had my time with the magic, but I'm past that now. Long past. Now it's been handed to you and you alone. Not me, not Paul, just you."

"But Paul doesn't mind. He wants to help," Celia said.

"No, it's not right." Her grandmother shook her head. "You'll just have to think of another way."

"But there is no other way." Celia wanted to cry. Oh why did her grandmother have to ruin her plans? She and Paul had it all worked out. "This is the best way, Grammy. Paul's right there. It will be easy for him."

"It's not Paul's problem," Grammy said. "It's yours, and you need to handle it yourself. If there's going to be trouble, you need to take responsibility for it. Doing the right thing isn't always easy, but it's always right. Remember that."

Celia didn't argue, but she knew her solution was the only one. Paul was right there in the house. It would be nothing for him to go into his aunt's room while she slept and take the flute off her nightstand. Then he'd give it to Celia and it would be done. Easy peasy. There was no other way to do it. For the first time ever, she was going to go against her grandmother's wishes.

CHAPTER TWENTY-TWO

*C*elia didn't get a chance to talk to Paul until the bus ride home the next day. He settled in next to her, banging his backpack against her feet. "Did you get the flute?" Celia asked.

Paul didn't say anything, but the look on his face said it all. "Yeah, well, don't get mad, Celia..." He tapped his fingers on his knee and didn't meet her eyes. "I was gonna take it yesterday, really I was gonna, but it didn't work out."

"Why not?"

"I know I said I'd help you and stuff, but I can't now. We can still be friends though, right, Celia? You aren't mad at me, are you?"

"I don't get it. Why didn't you get the flute for me? You promised you would." The bus lurched, and Celia grabbed onto the seat ahead of her. Toward the front of the bus some of the older kids were playing keep-away with some poor kid's baseball cap.

Paul wouldn't look her in the eye. "My aunt's being really, really nice now. My mom says I have to be extra good, cause she's going to help us with a problem. Something bad is going on with the government and my house, and my aunt said she'd make it stop. So I can't do anything to make her mad. I promised my mom I'd be good."

"Paul, this is really important to me. That flute was my Grammy's when she was my age. Your aunt stole it from us."

"I know, Celia." Paul hung his head. "I'm sorry. But hey—" He looked up suddenly, wide-eyed and hopeful. "Maybe you could get another flute somewhere. A better one, even."

"You don't understand, Paul." Celia turned toward the window so he couldn't see the tears forming in her eyes. What was she going to do now? Mira was counting on her to get the flute.

"Don't be mad, Celia." Paul leaned so close she could feel his breath on her neck. He felt terrible, that was obvious. She knew she should tell him it was okay, not to worry about it, but she just didn't have it in her. When they got to her stop, Paul got up to let her out. "Bye, Celia," he said sadly. All she could manage back was a very small wave.

CHAPTER TWENTY-THREE

*C*elia spent the next two days thinking of ways to retrieve the other half of the flute from around Vicky McClutchy's neck. She considered offering to buy it back, which was not a bad idea except for the fact that she didn't have much money. Next she thought of asking to see it, and then grabbing it and running away. A good plan, but Celia doubted Vicky would let her get close enough to hold it. She also envisioned setting off some kind of huge and terrible distraction like a smoke bomb, and then jumping onto a chair and lifting the necklace over Vicky's head during the ruckus. But when she really thought it through, none of these scenarios was likely to work. Oh, if only Paul hadn't changed his mind! She thought back bitterly to all the times she'd played his stupid games. All the hours doing what *he* wanted, and when she'd asked for just one teeny, tiny favor, would he do it for her? No.

The only thing that consoled her was that nothing had happened in two days. No dreams, no visits from Vicky McClutchy, no problems at Lovejoy World. Just school and homework and her grandmother's good cooking at dinnertime. Everything was fine. Maybe Mira was wrong and it was a false alarm. Her grandmother had said Mira could be a bit of a drama queen.

The second evening, as her family sat at the dinner table enjoying Grammy's roast chicken, creamed potatoes, and sweet corn, there was a knock at the door. Her father stopped halfway through his story about his latest new invention, a puppet theatre that came with materials for children to create their own puppets or marionettes. The family looked toward the front hall, wondering who was on the porch. They rarely got visitors in the evening. "I'll see who it is," Celia said, sliding off her chair and padding toward the door in her stocking feet. Behind her, Dad continued the conversation, explaining that he'd given a prototype of his new puppet theater set to a first grade teacher, and the kids had loved it. "It's the perfect toy," he said. "It allows for creativity and endless hours of fun. I can't wait to perfect it and get it out there for children to play with." As he talked, his voice got louder and faster, the way it always did when he was excited about a new toy.

Celia stood on tiptoe and looked through the small window at the top of the door. On the other side stood a tall man wearing a black coat and a brimmed hat. She didn't know him. "Little girl, I need to talk to Jonathan Lovejoy," the man said, putting his mouth close to the glass.

"Dad," Celia called out. "It's for you. A stranger." She'd been warned about strangers and wouldn't have opened the door for anyone she didn't know, especially not this man, who looked a little dangerous with his squinty eyes and pointy teeth.

Her father came quickly, followed by her mother and grandmother. He opened the door and greeted the stranger with a smile. "Hi, what can I do for you?"

"You're Jonathan Lovejoy?" the man asked with a mean smile. Celia got a bad feeling in the pit of her stomach.

"I am indeed." The man thrust a large envelope at her father. "What's this about?" Celia's father asked, taking it and looking it over.

"You've been officially notified of county business," the man said. "I'm going to testify to the board that I delivered this official document to you personally." He turned quickly and headed down the walkway to his car, which was parked out front.

"But what's this about?" her father called out.

The man didn't answer, just kept going. Celia watched as he got behind the wheel of his car and drove off into the night.

"What is it, Jonathan?" her mother asked.

"I'm not sure." Dad took his reading glasses out of his shirt pocket, flipped them open, and put them on. Celia and her mother and grandmother watched as he ripped the envelope open and pulled out a thick wad of paper.

"Why, that's our house," her mother said as he pulled out a large, glossy photograph. Her father flipped through the rest of the papers, all of them official looking with stamps and seals and large scrawly signatures at the bottom of each page.

They stood silently while Celia's father read one of the pages, his face a mixture of confusion and anger. "This can't be right," he said. "There must be some mistake."

"What is it, Jonathan?" Celia's grandmother rested a hand on his shoulder.

"According to this, the county is seizing our property so they can build a highway through this area." He read aloud: "You will be fairly compensated with payment to equal double the amount of the fair market value of your home. You have thirty days to vacate the premises. On that date, the sheriff's department will evict any remaining persons and your possessions will be removed and sold at auction."

"This has to be some kind of joke," her mother said.

"I don't think it's a joke." Celia's father rifled through the papers. "This looks very official." He frowned and pointed. "Why am I not surprised to see that Vicky McClutchy is one of the board members who signed these documents? It figures."

"But they can't do this!" Her mother twisted her hands nervously. "This can't be legal. There's no way we'd just go along with this. There has to be a way to fight this."

Her father sighed. "Of course we'll fight this. I'll call Brad tonight." Brad had been her father's college roommate. He was also an attorney and handled all the legal papers for Lovejoy World. Celia had often heard her parents talk about how smart Brad was. "If anyone can figure a way out of this, it will be Brad."

Grammy came over to Celia and gave her shoulder a slight squeeze. When Celia looked up, her grandmother gave her a nod and mouthed the word *flute*. It was obvious they needed magic now more than ever. The thought weighed heavily on Celia, who still felt confused about the whole thing and wondered why it all fell on her. What did she know about legal matters and seizing property? She looked up to her mother for some reassurance.

"Let's not worry about this now," Mom said in a false, chipper way. "It's probably going to turn out to be nothing." She smiled at Celia. "We should go finish dinner before it gets cold."

CHAPTER TWENTY-FOUR

That night, sometime after Celia had been tucked into bed, she left her room and went out to the landing to listen. Sitting there cross-legged with her back against the wall, she overheard her grandmother say good night to her parents before heading off to her own bedroom. After Grammy's door clicked shut, Celia knew her mother and father would feel free to talk.

"Finally," her mother said, "I thought your mother would never go to bed."

"Shh." This was her father. "Let's keep it down. Little pitchers have big ears."

"Celia's been asleep for hours," her mother said. "She was yawning before her head hit the pillow." Celia smiled. Her acting had worked.

"I don't want to upset her," her father said, "but Brad didn't have good news." Immediately after dinner, he'd locked himself into his home office to call attorney Brad. The conversation lasted an hour, and when he came out of the room, he looked shaken. Still he'd smiled and told them not to worry, Brad would handle it.

"What did he say?" her mother asked.

"It seems there's this old law on the books that makes it legal to seize private property under certain conditions. Something about the needs of the many superseding the rights of the few."

"I don't understand." Celia heard the scrape of a kitchen chair against the tile and pictured her mother sitting down at the table. "What does that mean?"

"It means that a greater number of people will benefit from having the highway go through than live in this house." Now her father pulled out a chair and sat.

"How can they just kick us out of our own house and tear it down for a road? Why can't they just build the highway somewhere else?" Her mother's voice had the sound of crying in it. "It's our house. Our house." She slammed her hand on the table. "We'll fight this. They can't really do it if we object, can they?"

"Actually, Brad says they can." Her father sighed. "They plan to raze the house and bulldoze the woods and put the highway right through here. He says we can appeal and that will put it off for a month or so, but it's impossible to overturn it. We could try to change the law, but that would take more time than we have."

Now her mother *was* crying. "Vicky McClutchy is behind this, I know it. She's doing this because we won't sell her the company. She's a vile, wicked, jealous person. She's barely human. I hate her."

Her father moved his chair closer and was making the soothing sound that Celia always found so comforting when she awoke from a bad dream. Her mother, however, was having none of it. "How can you be so calm?" she snapped. "We need to figure out a way to stop this."

"Believe me—I understand where you're coming from. Brad's going to investigate some more and look for loopholes. If there's a way around this, he'll figure it out. Until then, there's not much we can do. It won't help to get all emotional about this."

"I'm sorry I'm being so *emotional*," her mother said, sounding furious. "Sorry that I'm getting so upset about someone forcing us out of our home."

Her father said nothing. Celia wondered if he was counting to ten, the way he taught her to do whenever she felt like saying something mean. Finally he spoke. "I'm taking care of it the best way I know how, Michelle."

"You better fix this," her mother said. "Because this is all your fault. You and that Vicky McClutchy and your stupid feud from grade school. Honestly, it's hard to believe you can't remember what you did to make her so angry. If you'd just apologized at the time, none of this would have happened."

A cold draft passed Celia's way, and she hugged her knees and shivered. Her parents never argued; in fact, they rarely disagreed. She waited to hear her father's answer, but it never came. When she heard her mother get up from the table, Celia moved quietly back to her room and crawled under the covers. She had a feeling sleep that night would not come easily.

CHAPTER TWENTY-FIVE

*T*he mood in Celia's house changed after that. Her parents were oddly quiet the next morning. Her father, who usually whistled as he poured his coffee, was silent, and her mother neglected to wish Celia a good day as she headed out the door to the bus. Only her grandmother was her usual self. Even after Celia had filled her in on the bad news, Grammy remained cheerful. "It will all work itself out, I suppose," she said with a smile. Celia wasn't so sure.

On the playground at recess Paul took her aside to tell her that his family had gotten a similar envelope with the same news about their property. "But my Aunt Vicky said she'll fix it for us. She was against it, but they made her sign it, she said. My mom doesn't believe her, but my dad says if we gots to move, at least we'll have enough money to buy a bigger, better house. Maybe even one with a pool. Wouldn't that be cool, Celia? I'd invite you over for sure, okay? It would be fun to go swimming." Paul was so clueless.

After school Celia headed out to the woods, intending to talk to the only one who could help—Mira. Magic was the only answer, she was certain of that. When she reached the center of the Triple Trees, she stood in the exact spot where she'd first met the fairy girl. She'd brought her half of the flute and was just lifting it to her lips when a spot of light appeared in the distance. It moved fast, much faster than last time. Mira appeared in front of her as quickly as a camera flash. She came alone this time and looked irked. "I'm not a dog, you know. I don't come when you whistle." Mira hovered in midair and folded her arms.

"I'm sorry," Celia said, lowering the flute to her side, "but you came the last time I used the flute."

"I came the last time because I wanted to come and I knew you'd be here, not because you called me."

"Oh."

Mira flew in dizzying circles around Celia. When she finally stopped in front of Celia, her grouchiness had vanished and she was smiling. "Why so serious, young one? Things not going well for you?"

"Things are terrible," Celia said, and proceeded to tell Mira about the papers from the county and the plans to tear down the house and destroy the woods. "And now my mother is angry with my father and everything is awful."

"Well, you're right, that is terrible," Mira said. "What are you planning on doing about it?"

"Me? I can't do anything. I'm just a girl." Didn't Mira understand how limited she was? Celia didn't know anything about government business. Her parents wouldn't even let her use the stovetop unless they were around to supervise. "I thought you could do something with your magic. Make the county board change their minds or put a force field around the house or something."

"A force field." Mira scoffed. "As if. Someone's been watching too many movies. I can't create force fields."

"Okay, then what about making them change their minds? Maybe put the highway somewhere else?" This sounded reasonable to Celia. Changing the minds of a bunch of boring grownups should be a cinch for someone who could infiltrate dreams and fly.

"Fairy folk don't practice mind control. We give suggestions and guidance only." Mira recited this like she was reading from a rule book. "Honestly."

"Okay then, what *can* you do to help?"

Mira flitted up and down, moving so fast that she was as transparent as a soap bubble. She finally landed on Celia's shoulder. "You have more power than you know," she whispered in her ear.

Celia had heard that before but still wasn't sure what it meant, so it wasn't too helpful. "Just tell me what I should do," she said.

"I already told you the last time we met here. The key is the flute." Mira kept her balance by holding on to a strand of Celia's hair. "Have you recovered the missing part yet?"

"No, but I know where it is. Vicky McClutchy has it, and she keeps it on a chain around her neck."

"Good, you found it!" Mira did a little dance step. "Okay, first you go get it. Once the two parts are combined, then you'll really have something. Pay attention now, and I'll tell you how it all works. You take the two pieces out to the Watchful Woods, because that's where the magic is strongest. Once you get there, you put the two pieces together and blow into the flute. Trust me, you'll know if it's working. Then, you make your wish. If you make the right wish, all your problems are solved. Easy peasy. All you have to remember are the three rules of the flute. The first is—"

"Wait!" Celia said. "I'm not sure I'll be able to remember all the rules. Maybe I should go get some paper and a pen to write this down."

"A smart girl like you? You'll remember. There's only three of them," Mira said. She ticked off on her fingers. "Number one, no wishing for more wishes. Two, you can't force someone to do what they don't want to do. Three, the wish has to bring a good outcome for everyone involved. See, simple."

It didn't sound simple to Celia. A good wish, in her opinion, would force the board to change their minds about the highway or make Vicky McClutchy disappear from the planet Earth. She was pretty sure neither of these fit with the rules. "How can I ever come up with a wish that will fix everything *without* forcing people *and* have a good outcome for everyone?" she said, blinking back tears of frustration. "Your rules make it impossible."

Mira flew up and gently stroked her cheek. "Others have done it, and you can too. Don't think about it too much, or you'll make yourself crazy. Wish with your heart and not your head."

Celia didn't have much confidence in the wisdom of her heart. "I wish you'd just tell me what to do. I came to you for help."

"I am helping," Mira said. "You just don't see it yet. Go and get the flute; the rest will follow."

"But I told you already, I can't get it," Celia said. "Vicky McClutchy keeps it on a chain around her neck. I've already thought of everything I can do to get it back, and there's nothing that will work. I need help."

"Find out when she's not wearing it. That'll be your chance."

"But she always wears it, except when she's sleeping," Celia said.

"That's when you get it then," Mira whispered into her ear. "Wait until she's asleep."

"But I can't do that," Celia cried out, but Mira was already spiraling away from her. "Wait, come back!"

As Mira became a speck of light off in the distance, Celia heard a small voice in her head say, "You're a smart girl. You'll figure out a way to get it back."

CHAPTER TWENTY-SIX

*T*hat evening during dinner there was another knock on the door. Her parents exchanged a worried look. "I'll get it," Celia said, putting down her napkin.

"No, stay here," said her father, getting up. "I'll handle this." At the table everyone was quiet. They heard the door opening and him saying, "What do *you* want?" in an angry way.

Celia's mother got up to see what was happening, and Grammy and Celia followed. On the other side of the screen door, they saw Vicky McClutchy, dressed in a business suit and holding a briefcase. Her earrings looked like large, shiny buttons. "I want to help you," she was saying to Celia's father.

Celia could only see her father's back, so she couldn't read his expression, but there was no mistaking the anger in his voice. "You have a lot of nerve coming to my home after what you've pulled." Vicky tried to say something, but he wouldn't let her. "If you have something to say, contact my attorney. I'm not falling for your tricks ever again. There's nothing you can say that I want to listen to." He stopped to catch his breath and turned to Celia's mother, who looked stricken. His face was flushed, and the tips of his ears were bright red. "I'd like you to leave right now."

"All right then, if you don't want to hear my idea for letting you keep your house, I'll just leave." Vicky smirked and turned away. Her high heels made a click-click noise on the walkway as she headed toward her car.

"I've wanted to tell that woman off for years," Celia's father said. "But I've always been the better person. Well, that day is over."

Celia's mother craned her neck to get a better view of Vicky's departure. "Maybe we should have listened to what she had to say. We could call her back." She gave him a pleading look.

Her father was incredulous. "You've got to be kidding me."

"But she said she could help us keep our house, Jonathan."

He harrumphed and shut the door. "I'm sure her plan involves us handing over Celia or selling our souls to the devil. Trust me, it was nothing we'd want to do."

And he was right. After dinner, and a lengthy heated argument between her parents, Celia's mother went into the den to call Vicky McClutchy. She came out shaking her head.

"So what's her brilliant plan for saving our house?" her father asked.

"She says she'll call off the whole deal if we sell her our company." Her mother began sobbing, which made Celia cry too. Instinctively, her father went to hug her mother, while Grammy pulled Celia close. The unhappiness in the house was taking over. "What did you tell her?" her father asked tenderly.

Celia's mother sniffed. "I told her to just forget it. We aren't selling. When I think about all our employees—why, they're like family! How could we do that to them? Unimaginable." She wiped her eyes. "But then I think about this house that's been in your family for generations...it's our home, Jonathan! I can't imagine not living here. Not hanging Celia's Christmas stocking on the fireplace mantel in the living room. Not eating together in our cozy kitchen. Not..." Here she broke down crying and pressed her face against his chest.

Celia had her own list of horrible unimaginables. She couldn't imagine saying good-bye to the balcony off her bedroom, or not having the staircase landing that allowed for her nighttime excursions. How would she live without the woods behind her house, and what would happen to Mira and the rest of the fairies when the bulldozers came through?

"Now, now," Grammy said, interrupting the misery. "Let's not get too anxious about this. Most of the time people worry for nothing. It will probably all work itself out."

Celia's father said, "I wish you were right, Mom, but this time I think we should be prepared for the worst. Brad says it looks like we'll have to move."

That night, listening from the landing, Celia overheard her father say, "Maybe we *should* consider selling the company."

"Jonathan, how can you say that?!" her mother said.

"It's just that my mother and Celia will be crushed if we have to move. Did you see the look on our daughter's face?" He sighed. "And you know, I was thinking, if we sell Lovejoy World, we can turn around and start a new company. We'll call it something else, get a new building, and hire back all our employees. What do you say? It could work."

Her mother exhaled, loud and weary. "Except Vicky McClutchy would still own the rights to the name 'Lovejoy World,' which is *our* name, and she'd own all the toys and games you've created. All your ideas, they'd be hers. Look at *The Good Deed Game*, for example. Just one of your many inventions, but how many good deeds have come from that one game? We've heard from thousands of people who say it inspired them to do good deeds in real life. You did that, Jonathan. You and you alone. All the joy and all the good you've brought into the world. Don't let her take that away."

Celia's father shook his head. "I just don't know what else to do. I've never had a problem I couldn't solve before. Even Brad thinks it's hopeless." Complete silence. If Brad thought it was hopeless, that was it. "I think we're stuck, Michelle. We're out of options. We're going to lose our house."

Celia crawled back into bed just before midnight, exhausted. The sun came through her window before she was ready, but she still had to get up. It was a school day, and if she wasn't standing out front when the bus came, it left without her.

CHAPTER TWENTY-SEVEN

$\mathcal{U}$nder the silvery light of a full moon, Mira lined up the other fairies for an important briefing. "We all stick together tonight," she barked. "There's safety in numbers. You *never* go off by yourself, unless you want to get eaten by a shadow thing." For emphasis, she pointed at each one in turn. She didn't want to tell them she spoke from personal experience. Her encounter with the shadow thing the time she'd been saved by the original Celia was fresh in her mind. Even after all these years, she remembered the rotten-meat stench of the fake coyote's breath and the feel of his teeth grazing her legs. That thing had exuded wickedness.

"What are we supposed to do?" asked one of the younger fairies, a pipsqueak named Pim.

"You aren't supposed to do anything. This mission belongs to me and Jasmine. The rest of you are just coming along as backup." Honestly, these new ones were unbelievable. "Jasmine!"

Jasmine stepped forward. "I'm here." She had the eager look of someone who didn't realize how serious this night would be. How well she did her job would affect the entire future of the fairies of the woods, and maybe the rest of the world. It was always risky putting so much responsibility on someone so new. Jasmine had just taken over at that boy Paul's house. Boyd was such a nincompoop he didn't even care that he was replaced. Most fairies would have felt great shame, but not Boyd. The higher-ups put him in charge of a house on the other side of the woods where a single, retired man lived. By himself. Completely alone. Most of the time the man watched TV or slept. There wasn't much Boyd could mess up there.

"Jasmine, you know your part?" Mira squinted. Jasmine looked particularly bright and shiny tonight. Her wings glimmered, and the moon shone on her hair.

"Yes, I know my part. I'm ready."

"Okay then," Mira said. "Everyone stay close and think good thoughts. We're heading out."

CHAPTER TWENTY-EIGHT

*A*ttorney Brad came over after dinner the next evening. The adults pored over paperwork at the kitchen table and discussed what they now were calling "the situation." Celia lurked nearby but only caught snatches of the conversation. Brad told her parents that reversing the situation was nearly impossible. They could appeal if they wanted to, but he doubted it would help. Their house would eventually be torn down, no matter what. Celia's parents looked gloomy after he'd left, but they went through the motions of family life as usual, tucking her in and turning on her nightlight before kissing her good night.

She waited one hour after her parents went to bed, then got up and changed into jeans, a T-shirt, and sneakers. She opened the balcony doors and tiptoed outside to the railing. Good, a full moon. At least it wasn't completely dark. "Mira," she called out softly, "I'm going to get the flute tonight." The quiet echoed back at her. There was no way to know for sure if Mira had heard her. Returning to her room, she tucked the half flute into her back pocket for luck.

Celia slowly made her way down the stairs, hugging the wall and avoiding the one creaky step. The house was so quiet she could hear the wind whistling outside. When she reached the kitchen, a ghostly form standing alongside the back door startled her. She jumped, just about to yell, when she recognized her grandmother holding out her sweatshirt jacket. "You'll need this," Grammy said softly.

"Thanks," Celia said, pulling it over her head.

Grammy kissed her cheek and opened the back door. "Good luck," she said, with a smile in her voice. "Be careful."

"I will." Celia took a deep breath and headed out, hesitating on the patio to look back at her grandmother. This was crazy. Even with the moonlight, it was too dark and too late for a girl her age to be out alone. Surely her grandmother would call her back in?

Instead, Grammy whispered from the doorway, "I'll keep the door unlocked so you can get back in."

Celia nodded and headed down the path toward Paul's house. The wind whipped around her, whistling with a thin, slippery voice. *Go home*, it said. *Too dangerous.* A hard gust made her shudder. *Something will get you!*

No. She wasn't listening. *Wouldn't* listen. She kept walking, following the route she'd traveled so frequently she instinctively knew when to step over roots and when to avoid low, muddy spots. She wouldn't turn back until she had the flute in her hand. A cloud moved over the moon, darkening the path and making her halt, but only for a moment. The wind picked up and said, with a ghostly whisper, *Little girls shouldn't be out at night. What if your parents find out?*

"They won't find out," she said aloud.

But what if they do? You'll be in BIG trouble.

She ignored the wind and spoke quietly to herself. "I'm just going to Paul's to get the flute. Once I have it, I'll come straight home." It wasn't really trespassing. She'd been in Paul's house so many times, she was practically a member of the family. And taking the flute wasn't stealing because it really belonged to her grandmother. If anything, she was just righting a wrong, and that was a good thing.

The wind blew harder, making her hair fly upwards. *What if Vicky McClutchy catches you? You'll be one sorry little girl.*

"Oh go away," she said. "You're stupid." Her heart was pounding now, but she continued, clambering up the small incline that led to Paul's. When the house came into view, she stopped to catch her breath. The house was a two-story like hers, sided with wooden clapboard. Unlike Celia's place, none of the outside lights were on. Darkness was good for staying undetected. Not so good for finding your way.

As Celia walked to the front of the house, she stuck her hands in her pockets and found something smooth and cylindrical. Something that wasn't there the last time she wore the jacket. A mini-flashlight. She pulled it out and pushed the button, producing a thin shaft of light. She exhaled and said a silent thank-you to her grandmother.

At the front door she paused and lifted the welcome mat, looking for the house key that was always there. Except it wasn't. She got down on her hands and knees to look closer, and she ran her hands over the surface, even checking under the nearby flower pot stuffed with plastic geraniums.

No key. Now what?

She stood for a moment, out of ideas, and the wind said, *Well, that's it then. Time to go home, little girl. Good effort and all that.*

"No," she said and walked to the end of the porch to peer into the living room window. The moon was still cloud covered, so she couldn't see much inside. Celia put the flashlight between her teeth and pushed on the window sash in the hope it was unlocked. No such luck. Stuck tight.

As she worked at getting the window open, the flashlight spotlighted Clem, the sleepiest dog in the world. Poor goofusy, fast-asleep Clem. He didn't even stir when someone was trying to break into the house at night.

An inner voice made her pause. *Try the dog door.* She lifted her head and listened. *In back. Go to the back of the house and go through the doggie door.* The suggestion was inside her head and somehow all around her at the same time. It came from Mira.

Celia used the flashlight to illuminate her path. A chilly breeze followed her steps on the spongy grass. Now she was within sight of the back door with its swinging Clem-sized door. She dropped down, lifted the flap, and looked right into the kitchen. Incredible. Could it really be that easy?

Behind her the wind tried to discourage her. *Go back! You don't belong here!* And then Mira's voice: *Block out that voice. It's just a cowardly shadow thing. You have the strength to do what needs to be done. I believe in you.*

Celia understood then, and when the shadow thing disguised as the wind spoke up again, she ignored it and with one quick movement scrambled through Clem's door.

She let her eyes adjust and used the small flashlight to find her way. It was eerie being inside Paul's house at night,

Karen McQuestion

when she wasn't supposed to be there. On the way to the staircase, she glanced into the living room and saw Clem still sleeping, his stomach rising and falling in rhythm with his snores.

Celia clicked off the light and headed stealthily up the stairs. Although her heart pounded in her chest, she managed to stay in control of the situation by reminding herself the whole ordeal would be over in half an hour. Soon enough she'd have possession of the flute, and after that she'd be back in her own bed.

At the top of the stairs she took a quick look around. The door to Paul's parents' room at the end of the hallway was closed. Good. She tiptoed over to Paul's room, where the door was wide open and a mega-bright nightlight illuminated his sleeping form. And here he had made fun of her fear of the dark. Ha! She watched him for a moment, studying his slow breathing and the way he hugged something that looked like a stuffed animal.

Working her way down the hall, she came to the guest bedroom, currently occupied by Vicky McClutchy, the woman who had made Celia's mother cry and her parents fight. The one who wanted to knock down their house. The very same person who would destroy the woods, given the chance. That door was open a crack, thank goodness. Celia just might be able to come and go without Vicky ever knowing she'd been there. Celia didn't have to turn on the light to know the layout of the room: a bed, a dresser, a nightstand, and not much room in between the three. It was a very small room. The nightstand, which is where Paul said his aunt put the flute at night, was on the far side of the bed,

108

which meant Celia would have to go all the way around to get to it.

Celia carefully pushed the door with one finger, wincing as it creaked open. She peeked around the doorframe to see Vicky sleeping faceup, her fingers folded together on top of the covers. She was still as a statue until she let out an unladylike snort and mumbled something. Celia froze.

"Gerber samse reebie," Vicky said. Celia waited stock-still as Paul's aunt shifted onto her side, away from the door. The next words the sleeping woman uttered came out clearly. "We used to be best friends." Her voice was so small and sad, she sounded more like a little girl than a grown woman. Vicky sighed and then started snoring loudly.

Celia crouched down and crawled around the bed, inching closer and closer to the nightstand. The carpeting did a good job muffling the sound of her movements. Slowly, slowly. Just a few more minutes and she'd have the prize within her grasp.

She baby-crawled to the other side of the bed. Right hand, left knee, left hand, right knee, over and over again, so slowly and silently she might have been a wisp of air crossing the room. On the bed above her Vicky snored, and outside the wind wailed, but Celia wasn't afraid of either one anymore, because now the nightstand was right in front of her. She was nearly home free. Just a little more.

Moving cautiously, she slid her hand up the front of the nightstand until her fingertips reached the top. She patted the surface until her hand made contact with the chain. Sweet victory! She pinched the chain between her fingers. Now she had it.

"Bess frens," Vicky mumbled and dropped her arm over the side of the bed so that it rested on Celia's back. "Heel ree sary." Celia choked back a gasp and kept herself steady. Now what? If she pulled away, the motion would certainly wake Vicky. But if she didn't move, she could be stuck there all night and discovered in the morning. She kept rigid for a few minutes waiting to see if Vicky would shift positions on her own, but if anything, the woman's arm got heavier on Celia's back. Something had to be done and soon, because now Celia's outstretched arm was tired and her legs were getting numb.

Celia had just let go of the chain and put her hand down on the floor when she heard a loud thudding noise downstairs. She tilted her head to listen. There it was again, thumping its way across the house, slamming itself against the walls and now scrambling up the stairs. Thud, thud, thud. And then, a mournful, plaintive howl. Clem? The dog had never sounded like this in all the times she'd been to Paul's. In fact, Clem had rarely been conscious when she was around. He was more of a dog-shaped floor pillow than anything else. Could it really be Clem coming up the stairs?

Yes, she recognized the rarely heard sound of tags clanking and the click of his toenails against the hardwood floor in the hallway. Now Clem was yelping loudly and coming this way. This was not good.

Vicky stirred and then sat up, wide awake and angry. "What the—?" She faced the door, so she wasn't looking in Celia's direction, but still, it was only a matter of time before Celia was found out, and that would mean big trouble.

CHAPTER TWENTY-NINE

*T*he fairies clustered together in the trees behind Paul's house. "This is your part," Mira told Jasmine. Up until this point, Mira had run the show, guiding Celia through the woods and encouraging her through the house. One of the younger fairy boys, Jameel, had interrupted at one point, questioning her tactics. He'd asked if it was really such a good idea to encourage the girl to trespass. Foolish boy. As if she could stop to answer such a complex question when they were in the middle of something this big and important. Now she focused on the fledgling, Jasmine. "Are you ready?"

"But I don't know what to do!" Jasmine said, the panic evident in her voice. "Can't you do it for me this time? I'll pay attention and then next time I'll know better."

Mira sympathized with Jasmine's fear but also knew you couldn't put off your responsibility to another fairy. She reached out and grabbed the younger fairy's shoulders, making her wings tremble. "Snap out of it. We've practiced this plenty of times. You know you can do this." Goodness gracious, now the girl looked like she was going to cry.

That wouldn't do. Mira softened her tone. "Okay, let's just take this one step at a time. You already took care of the parents and they're in a deep sleep. Now close your eyes and think of the boy, Paul. What is he doing?"

Jasmine sniffed and cooperated. With eyes shut tight, she answered, "He's hugging his panda and dreaming."

"Dreaming of what?" Mira coaxed.

"Paul's dreaming of swimming on a sunny day. He's floating on his back, feeling so happy and peaceful. He's paddling around." She herself sounded relaxed now, which wasn't good. It didn't help to get too caught up in human dreams. Jasmine's arms waved at her sides, like she was swimming. The other fairies, especially the younger ones who didn't have a family yet, watched enthralled.

"Pay attention now. This next part is important," Mira said. "Slide into his dream, but don't let him see you. Let him know he's dreaming and he needs to wake up and go to his aunt's room across the hall. Tell him Celia needs his help."

Jasmine scrunched her forehead in concentration. Her fairy glow intensified and brightened so that all of them were enveloped in love light. This girl really had the gift, Mira thought. Such an improvement over that loafer, Boyd. Maybe, with Jasmine's help, Paul's house could become a happy place after all. "I'm telling him," Jasmine said, and smiled. "He hears me."

"Is he waking up?" Mira asked. Time was critical. She sensed poor Celia was crouched next to the bed not knowing what to do. She was holding up well for now, but she needed help. It was clever of the shadow things to rile up the dog, but it would take more than that to ruin the whole mission, if she had anything to say about it.

Jasmine shook her head. "He's confused. He says he doesn't want to wake up, and he doesn't want to go near his aunt's room. He says he'll see Celia tomorrow."

Mira was afraid of this. "Sometimes this happens," she said, keeping her voice steady. "But you know what to do, right?"

Jasmine's light faded. She knew what she needed to do, but it wouldn't be pleasant. "I have to jerk him awake."

"That's right." They'd covered this many times during fairy training. There were different strategies depending on the dream. If the person was walking or running, the fairy often made them lose their balance. Then the dreamer would jerk themselves awake trying not to fall. For car dreams, they'd need to put on the brakes. Flying dreams would suddenly have obstacles like mountains or tall trees. Jerking someone awake was a basic skill but one that involved fairy creativity. "Can you do it?" Mira asked after a minute or so of silence.

"I already have." Jasmine smiled, and again she lit up from within. "He's up and heading out the door."

CHAPTER THIRTY

*S*omething in his dream had pulled Paul underwater, and he'd jerked awake fighting his way to the surface. In a panic, he jumped out of bed and ran into the hallway just in time to see Clem's back end disappear into the guest room. A moment later he heard Aunt Vicky yell, "What the—?" Paul peered in and saw Clem sitting on top of his aunt, licking her face.

"Get off of me!" Vicky screamed, swatting at the dog. Seeing Paul in the doorway, she said, "What's the big idea, letting your stupid mutt in here when I'm trying to sleep?"

"Sorry, Auntie," Paul said, reaching for Clem's collar. For some reason, he wasn't surprised to see Celia pop up on the far side of the bed. Had he heard something about this in his dream? It was hard to tell. His head was still foggy with sleep. Celia motioned for silence with one finger to her lips and held the flute necklace up in the air. He understood.

"Being sorry doesn't help," Vicky snapped, unaware that Celia was right behind her. "Just get him out of here." Her voice was so shrill and loud, it was amazing she hadn't awakened his parents.

Paul thought fast and said, "Sometimes Clem acts like this when something is happening outside. I thought I heard someone on the driveway doing stuff to your car."

"What?! Why didn't you say so?" Vicky threw back the covers and got out of bed. "Nobody better be messing with the Beemer." She pushed past Paul and Clem and ran down the hall to the stairway.

After they heard her clomping down the stairs, Celia got up from her hiding spot. "Thanks, Paul," she said quietly.

Paul pulled on Clem's collar. "You gotta move quick and get out of here. She's gonna come back, and my mom and dad might wake up any second," he whispered, gesturing for her to follow him. Celia put the necklace over her head and trailed Paul and Clem down the stairs.

"It's a good thing you came," Celia said breathlessly. "I didn't know what to do."

At the bottom of the stairs, Paul held out an arm to stop her. He peeked out the front window and said, "You have to go out the back, and we gotta move fast. Come with me."

The pair moved quickly through the house. Now Clem was following them, his nose nudging Celia's legs toward her escape. Paul unlatched the deadbolt, flipped the lock open, and turned the knob. "Thanks, Paul," Celia said softly and then, "I'm sorry I wasn't so nice before."

"It's okay." Paul jiggled the knob impatiently. "But you hafta hurry."

"Come over tomorrow," Celia said as she slipped through the door. "We can play whatever you want."

Paul didn't say anything, but he nodded before closing the door and locking her out in the cool night.

CHAPTER THIRTY-ONE

*C*elia let out a sigh of relief, turned on the flashlight, and aimed the light ahead of her as she walked. The breeze felt good after the stuffy air in Paul's house. How long had she been trapped on the floor next to the bed? Forever, it felt like. If Paul hadn't come along, she would have been discovered for sure.

Finally, finally, it was over. One half of the flute was in her pocket, and the other part hung around her neck. All she had to do was go into the woods to connect the two pieces and she could make a wish that would save her house and the woods that were home to the fairies. But that could wait until tomorrow. It was late and the path was dark, even with help from a flashlight and the moon. Deeper in the woods, the darkness got so thick it was suffocating. She had no desire to go there now. Tomorrow would be better.

Making the wish would be tricky, especially since she only got one. She thought about Mira's rules: *One, no wishing for more wishes. Two, she couldn't force someone to do what they don't want to do. Three, the wish had to bring a good outcome for everyone involved.* The rules were going to make it hard for her, but Mira said other people had successfully used the magic of the flute. Hopefully she'd figure out something.

She hummed as she went, careful not to trip or walk into brambles. Grammy had left the back door unlocked so she could slip in without waking the household. If her parents were awake, she could always say she'd heard something outside and went to investigate. They would be horrified, she knew that, and she'd get a good talking to, but there wouldn't be any serious consequences. Maybe grounding. She could live with that if it meant her home would be saved from the bulldozers.

Celia was halfway home when she heard the wind's shrill, whispery voice say, *Now you're going to get it!* She shut out the sound and trudged on, quickening her pace. As she trotted forward, she patted her pocket and then touched the chain around her neck, making sure both halves of the flute were still with her. The wind picked up with a fury, lifting her hair off her shoulders. It was then that she heard the sound of something running through the underbrush. A large animal coming right at her. Celia remembered her grandmother's story about the shadow thing disguised as a coyote, and felt a stab of fear. She ran faster, not looking back. From the noises behind her—the snapping of sticks and the yelping—she could tell it was getting closer. Terror-stricken, she had the urge to scream, but held back. It wouldn't help.

She turned off the flashlight and veered off the path into the woods, hoping the darkness would cover her. Outrunning it wasn't going to work. Maybe it would go past if it couldn't see her. She pressed her back against a tree and held her breath, waiting. The dark was her friend. It made her invisible.

The animal slowed and was nearby now, nosing around on the ground just a few yards away. Following her scent, most likely. Why hadn't she thought of that? The dark wouldn't help if the creature could find her by smell. "Mira," she called out softly. "Help me. I need your help." Nothing. Tears sprang to her eyes, and her breathing got harder. Could she hit the beast with the flashlight? Should she try to run away? The wind picked up and said, *I told you so. Little girls shouldn't be out at night by themselves.*

The animal shuffled on the other side of bush, and now she heard a familiar sound. The clinking of dog tags. Just then, Clem burst through the brush and jumped up to lick her face. "Clem," she said with relief, "what are you doing here?" Clem barked a response and wildly wagged his tail. He barked and barked, and she petted his head, wondering if the fairies had sent Clem to see her home safely. He was like a big furry guardian angel in a dog suit.

She stepped out onto the path, and Clem bounded after her. "I'm going home, boy," she said, rubbing behind his ears. "We have to be quiet now." Her steps were lighter with Clem by her side. She was sure the dog would go home on his own once she was safely inside her own house. Clicking on the flashlight, she continued down the path. Clem walked next to her, occasionally pausing to check out something of interest. Celia looked down, waving the light over the ground as she walked.

She was so preoccupied she didn't notice the other person in the woods, the one following her on the path. The one who reached out and grabbed her sweatshirt, yanking her off her feet. Celia dropped her flashlight and felt her stomach lurch when she came face-to-face with Vicky McClutchy.

"You little thief," Vicky said. "I bet you thought you'd get away with it. But I'm too smart for you. When I came back in the house, I heard the back door click, and there was Paul stammering like an idiot. Then when I went upstairs I noticed my necklace was gone. It didn't take much to figure it out." She let go with a forceful push, and Celia fell backwards onto the ground. Looking up, Celia saw the full moon behind Vicky's head, like a halo. An angry halo. "Luckily that stupid mutt led me right to you." Next to her, Clem barked happily, unaware of his role in this whole thing. "Now hand over my flute before I call the police and have you taken off to jail."

Celia covered the flute with her hand. "It's not your flute. It's belongs to my grandmother. She got it as a gift when she was a little girl."

Vicky threw back her head and laughed. "You are so wrong, little Lovejoy. It's mine and I can prove it. I've worn it continuously for nearly thirty years. Everyone knows it's my good luck charm. It's been in every photo of me since grade school." She leaned over and put her foot on Celia's stomach, holding her firmly in place. "I'll tell you what. I'm in a good mood. Hand it over right now, and I won't call the police." She smiled. "At least not tonight."

Celia swallowed hard, stuck on her back between Vicky McClutchy and the hard ground and not knowing what to do. Trapped. *This would be a really good time for some help,* she thought. *Mira, get me out of here.* Off in the distance an owl hooted and the wind roared, reminding her of every scary movie she'd ever seen. Fear settled into the pit of her stomach and she closed her eyes, hoping this was just a bad dream.

"Did you call?" Mira asked, and Celia looked up to see Mira and the other fairies clustered around Vicky's head and shoulders.

"Thank goodness you're here," she said, scooting out from under Vicky's foot.

"What are you talking about?" Vicky stumbled. Her concentration was broken as she regained her balance. It was only for a second, but it was enough.

"Run, Celia! Run!" Mira yelled. "Follow me." Celia scrambled to her feet and took off as fast as she could, not even watching where she was going, just following the cluster of fairies, who led the way with the glow of their light. She heard their small musical voices urging her on, and she plunged onward, trusting them to lead her to safety.

Deeper and deeper into the woods they went, but they couldn't quite lose Vicky, whose yelling could be heard in the background. "Come back here, you little brat. I'm not done with you yet."

Mira and the rest of the fairies led the way through the dark woods and didn't stop until they reached the space under the branches of the Triple Trees. Celia, who'd been right behind, came to a halt and leaned over to catch her breath. "I thought," she said panting, "we'd never lose her. Do you think we're safe here? Or do you think she'll find us?"

Mira peered down at Celia, a smile tugging at her lips. "She's not going to find *us*," she said. "She can't see fairies. You're the only one who can. But she's going to find you for sure. About two minutes from now. You can be certain of that."

Celia was puzzled. "But why are we here, then?" She looked around her trying to figure out an escape. With the fairies' help she might just make it out of there. "But there's still time to get away. Quick—if you show me the way home, I can maybe stay ahead of her." Even as she spoke, she heard Vicky and Clem thrashing through the underbrush. With every passing second they got closer.

Mira fluttered down in front of Celia's face. "I didn't bring you here to get away from Vicky McClutchy. I brought you here so you can make your wish."

"My wish?" Celia said. "But I'm not ready to do that yet. The rules are confusing, and I'm not really sure how it works. I was going to think about it some more and ask my Grammy for advice. I need more time."

Mira tapped the tip of Celia's nose. "You're over-thinking it. Wish with your heart and not your head."

Celia swallowed hard. "But what if my heart makes a mistake? If I do it wrong, the county will take my house and these woods will be turned into a highway." One of the other fairies gasped at this news, and Mira shot her a look of reproach.

"Don't worry about that," Mira said. "Just let your wish come from the heart, and everything will be fine. You can do this."

Celia took the chain off from around her neck and dug into her jeans pocket to get the other half of the flute. When Vicky burst into the clearing of the Triple Trees, she had a piece in each hand.

"I'm done playing games, little girl," Vicky said, roughly grabbing Celia by the arm. "I'm marching you straight home. Your parents are going to hear about this and so are the police. No one messes with Vicky McClutchy and gets away with it." Even in the dim light Celia could see that her face was contorted in anger, the kind of anger that was frightening. Vicky McClutchy looked like she wanted to kill the world.

As Vicky reached for the chain, Celia slammed the two parts together. When the two pieces met, they sparked like fireworks. The fairies twittered happily.

"What the—?" Vicky said, taking a step back. "How are you doing that?"

"It's magic," Celia said.

Vicky scoffed. "Like I'm going to believe that. I don't know what you're pulling, but it's not going to make a bit of difference, little girl." She stopped though, transfixed by the glorious colors of the light bouncing all around as the two pieces of the flute fused together. The sight of it filled Celia with joy, but it didn't seem to cheer Vicky up. Her face was still grim and unyielding. It struck Celia that Vicky wasn't a happy person, and that it must be awful to be her. She remembered what people said about Vicky McClutchy.

Vicky McClutchy is ruthless.

She never thinks of anyone but herself.

She's a vile, wicked, jealous person.

And then her grandmother's view: *Vicky McClutchy isn't bad, she's just misguided. She can only see things from her point of view, so she doesn't understand how her actions affect other people.*

Vicky jabbed at her with a sharp fingernail, interrupting her thoughts. "Give me back my flute," she said, her teeth bared.

Grammy's words—*she can only see things from her point of view*—echoed in Celia's brain, and suddenly she knew her wish. Lifting the flute to her lips, she softly breathed into the blowhole. Immediately, a stream of music swirled around her, filling her heart with joy. Oh, such a beautiful melody! She tingled with anticipation, like coming down the stairs first thing Christmas morning.

Then she spoke. "I wish," Celia said solemnly, "that Vicky McClutchy's heart will soften so she'll always feel how other people feel." She glanced up at Mira, who nodded approvingly.

Vicky jolted upright. Her eyes snapped shut, and she stood perfectly still. A few moments later, when she opened her eyes, her face had softened. The sharp chin and narrowed eyes had been replaced by an expression of wide-eyed wonder. To Celia, it looked as if the mean part of her personality had melted away, revealing a completely different sort of person underneath. "My goodness," Vicky said, glancing around the clearing, "It's awfully late for someone your age to be out in the woods. I bet you'd love to be home in bed right now."

*✳

CHAPTER THIRTY-TWO

*C*elia didn't fall asleep right away. She lay in bed for a long time, thinking over the night's events. Vicky McClutchy had walked her home, talking kindly to her the whole way. At first Celia thought it might be a trick. She waited for Vicky to revert back to her old self, snatching the flute away and threatening her again, but that never happened. Instead she asked questions about Paul. Celia found it easy to chat about Paul and their school. Vicky didn't seem to know much about her own nephew. She was surprised, for instance, to hear that Paul had a birthday coming up in a week. "What kinds of things does he like?" Vicky asked.

Celia shrugged. "The usual boy stuff, I guess. Big water guns and science kits and spy stuff. He said his mom might have his birthday party at a hotel pool so everyone could swim, but he said that last year and it didn't work out."

"Hmmm," Vicky said.

When they got to Celia's back door, Vicky leaned over and said, "Would you do me a favor? Could you tell your grandmother I'm sorry I had her flute for so long?"

"Okay, I will," Celia said, putting her hand on the knob.

Vicky said, "She was always so nice to me when I was a little girl. I used to come over here so much that this house was practically a second home for me."

This was news to Celia, who nodded and said, "Thanks for walking me home."

"You're welcome," she said. "I'm sorry if I scared you. I'm not sure what got into me. It's funny, but I feel completely different now." Vicky reminded Celia to lock up once she was inside, and they exchanged good-byes. Celia watched from the window and saw Vicky walk away with a spring in her step, her fingertips resting on Clem's head. It had been a long, peculiar night.

Later Celia dreamt Mira came into her room and whispered in her ear, "Well done, Celia. Tonight you have proven to be a brave and smart girl, outstanding in every way, every bit as special as your grandmother, the original Celia. The Watchful Woods fairies are forever grateful and will be at your service if ever there's a need."

The dream felt so real that when Celia woke up in the morning, she half expected the fairy girl to be sitting on her pillow. But she was alone, and it was Saturday. The sun had been up for a long while. Her alarm clock said ten o'clock, the latest she'd ever slept.

She put on her slippers and meandered downstairs, where she found her grandmother, parents, and Vicky McClutchy in the living room drinking coffee. "Here's our little sleepyhead," her mother said, setting down her mug and holding out her arms. "Come here, sweetie." Celia sat between her parents on the couch and took in the whole scene. Her heart thumped. Was Vicky here to tell her parents about last night? She hoped not.

"Celia, this lady is Vicky McClutchy," Grammy said. "She's Paul's aunt, and she went to school with your father."

"It's nice to meet you?" Celia said, her voice squeaky and unsure.

Vicky smiled. "I'm glad to meet you too. I saw you at the house with Paul the other day, but we weren't properly introduced."

"Vicky's not staying for long," her father said. "She just dropped in and said she had some good news. Your grandmother invited her in for coffee while I was taking out the garbage." He put his arm around Celia's shoulders. "Apparently Ms. McClutchy had some kind of epiphany last night." Celia recognized the sarcasm in his voice. She looked around the room and saw a different emotion on each adult's face. Her mother appeared hopeful, her father doubtful, and Vicky eager. Only her grandmother looked like her usual self, relaxed and open.

"What's an epiphany?" Celia asked.

"An epiphany is when you have a sudden understanding of something that hadn't been clear to you before," Grammy said. "It's a very good thing."

"A sudden understanding," Vicky said. "That's exactly what happened." She smiled shyly and took a sip of coffee.

"Please, don't make us wait any longer," her father said flatly. "We're all in suspense here."

"I couldn't sleep all night," Vicky said. "I realized that I've made some big mistakes, and I want to be a different person, a better person. I want to fix things I've done in the past. To start with, I'm going to reverse the county board's decision to seize your property for the new highway. Instead, we'll just expand the old highway on the other side of town. Your house and land won't be affected at all."

Celia's mother clasped her hands together. "Oh, thank goodness." She let out a sigh of relief.

Dad held up his hand. "Not so fast. What's the catch?"

"There's no catch."

He laughed. "Sorry to be skeptical, but you have a reputation for double-crossing. Let's just say I'll believe it when I see it."

Vicky's face fell, and it almost looked like, well—could it be that she blinked back tears? "I understand that given our past history you don't believe me, but I give you my word this time. Your house is safe. Not only that, but I'll make a motion to change the old law so it can't happen again."

"And in exchange for all this generosity, you want what?" Celia's father leaned forward and rested his hands on his knees. "A million dollars, my company, a kidney? What will it be, Vicky?"

"I only want one thing," Vicky said.

"Here we go," he said, turning to Celia's mother.

"I would like," she said, speaking slowly, "your forgiveness."

This was not what her father was expecting. The room was silent until Grammy said, "Forgiveness for what, dear?"

"For everything I've ever done to hurt you or anyone else. In the past I've been selfish and cruel. I realize that now. I can't undo the past, but if you will forgive me, Jonathan, I promise I will be different from now on."

Dad didn't say anything. Celia saw that he was trying to make sense of Vicky's remarkable transformation. It was hard for him to trust someone who'd never been trustworthy before.

Vicky said, "If you want some time to think it over, I understand."

Her father said, "Yes, I definitely need some time to process this."

Vicky looked like Paul did when Celia didn't want to come over after school anymore. "Okay."

Celia's stomach rumbled from hunger, but she didn't budge. She wasn't going to miss any of this. "Vicky, dear," her grandmother said, "didn't you say you brought something for Jonathan?"

"Oh yes." She reached down to open a canvas bag on the floor near her feet. "I have something that belongs to you, and I need to return it." She pulled out a large silver trophy the size of a blender. The top was a miniature replica of the planet Earth, revolving on an axis.

"The National Science Fair trophy?" her father said, his eyes widening.

"It really belongs to you. You won, fair and square," Vicky said. "I changed the judges' scorecards so I came out ahead. You were the real winner."

Her father stared, incredulous. "I knew it. I knew you did something. I just couldn't figure out what it was."

Vicky got up and handed the trophy to him. "I took the nameplate off. I'll have a new one made up with your name and information on it."

Her father tentatively fingered the Earth, making it spin. "But the records still list you as the winner that year."

"I know. I'm going to notify them and let them know I cheated so they can correct the records," Vicky said.

"You and McClutchy Toys are really well known. This will probably get picked up by the news media." Even as he talked, her father kept his eyes on the trophy.

"Yes, I've thought of that," Vicky said. "Once it gets out, everyone will know I cheated. It will make me look bad."

"Why do it then?" her father asked. "This was a long time ago. Except for me, there probably aren't many people who even remember or care about that science fair."

Vicky smiled, and this time it was a joyful smile. "I want to do it because it's the right thing to do. Doing the right thing isn't always easy, but it's always right." She turned to Grammy. "Isn't that what you used to always say?"

Grammy laughed. "I didn't know anyone was listening."

"I was listening," Vicky said. "It just took a long time to sink in. Better late than never, I guess."

The mood in the room had changed like the sun coming out after a storm. The conversation turned to more boring topics. Celia's grandmother talked about planting flowers now that the weather was warmer. Vicky and Celia's mother chatted about the neighborhood and how Celia and Paul's school had changed over the years. "When we went there, all the playground equipment was metal and there was gravel underneath. Remember how hot that slide got, Jonathan?" Vicky said, but Celia's father was so preoccupied with the trophy he could only murmur an affirmative. Celia put out a finger to touch it, and her father snapped out of his trance to give her a grin.

When the coffee mugs were empty, Vicky announced that she had to leave. "I need to go have a heart-to-heart talk with my sister and her family," she said. "Thank you for your hospitality and for allowing me to speak my piece."

"Thank you for your change of heart," Celia's mother said.

They all escorted her to the front door. Vicky had the empty canvas bag under one arm, while her father held his trophy. "You don't have your car here?" Grammy asked, peering out the front door.

"Oh no, I walked," Vicky said. "There's something nice about being out in the fresh air. It really clears your head, don't you think, Celia?" She winked. As quick as a static shock, there was a jolt of recognition between them, an affirmation of the secret they shared. *Last night really happened*, Celia thought happily. *I did all this. I fixed everything.*

Vicky was halfway down the walk when Celia's father suddenly rushed out the door after her. "Vicky, wait!" he yelled.

Celia watched as her father and Vicky exchanged a few words. When Vicky reached forward to shake hands, her father ignored the gesture and pulled her into a hug instead.

"What in the world is he doing?" her mother asked.

Grammy put an arm around Celia's shoulder and said, "He's forgiving her."

The look on his face when he returned to the house was one of pure jubilation. "Ladies," he said, coming in the door, "I think we have just witnessed a miracle."

CHAPTER THIRTY-THREE

*I*n the weeks afterwards, life settled back to normal. There were no more fairy sightings or dreams, and Celia's grandmother didn't seem very interested in talking about Mira and the fairy world.

Most upsetting, the flute, still on its chain, had disappeared. Celia searched everywhere, including the hiding space under the floorboards, but it was nowhere to be found. Her mother, the only one prone to tidying up and moving things, said she hadn't seen it. It had vanished. Grammy said the fairies had probably reclaimed it. After all, Celia had used her turn at the wishing magic, so it was no good to her anymore. But without the flute as proof, it sometimes seemed like her adventure in the woods had never happened at all.

Celia spent the first morning of summer vacation at Paul's watching a team of excavators dig an enormous hole in his backyard. One digging machine scooped up all the dirt to one side, while another lifted the pile into a large truck. A man, dressed in coveralls, stood between the two machines pointing and yelling instructions.

It was hard to imagine that in just a few weeks this crater would be an in-ground swimming pool with a water slide and diving board—a birthday gift to Paul from his aunt Vicky. "It's gonna cost thousands and thousands of dollars!" Paul had told Celia when he first got the news. "My mom choked on her iced tea when she heard."

The morning of the groundbreaking, Celia and Paul sat cross-legged just inside the patio door. A front row seat, said Paul's mother, and plenty close for the two of them. Paul would have preferred to be outside, right by the action, but his parents had decided it was far too dangerous.

By the time Celia's mother came to pick them up, the morning was over and the hole nearly finished. The two friends had eaten sandwiches and chips in their spot by the patio window just before noon. Watching had been fun at first, but for Celia, it had gotten monotonous. Now they were going to spend the afternoon at Lovejoy World, to see her father present his newest toy creation.

When they arrived, the factory was buzzing with excitement, but Celia's father wasn't in sight. Her mother left Paul and Celia with the employees in the main area and set off to find him. Today, folding chairs filled what was usually an open area, and a small table at the front held something covered with a white cloth. The workers waited excitedly for the great unveiling. In the meantime, they were laughing and talking and dancing to music. J.J., the boy who usually pushed the broom, was trying to juggle, without much success. Everyone was eager to find out about the company's new toy.

In the past, Mr. Lovejoy's announcements were always greeted with enthusiasm. Usually his ideas were developed with the help of everyone in the company, but this time, he and Manuel, the electronics wizard, had worked on it in secret. Even Celia's mother had no idea what they'd come up with. Celia overheard one of the plush department ladies say the anticipation was killing her.

"Hey, Celia," called out Marge. "Come here and sit with us. I baked your favorite." Celia and Paul went to sit in the front row, where they were handed brownies and cups of punch.

"This place is so cool," said Paul, chewing and swinging his legs.

"I told you," Celia said.

"Attention, everybody, attention!" Her father strode to the front of the room, followed by Manuel and her mother. J.J. dropped the juggling balls, and they bounced to the back of the room. Someone turned off the music.

"I want to thank all of you for being here today, and every day," said Dad, standing behind the table. "Without all of you wonderful people, there would be no Lovejoy World, and the kids of the world would be missing out on a lot of great toys and games." The room exploded in applause and cheering. Celia's father held up a hand for silence. "Today I asked you all here to see our newest toy. I was inspired by my daughter," here he bowed in Celia's direction, "and by a dream I had one night. My newest invention was built in honor of Celia." Marge reached over and squeezed Celia's arm, while Paul whispered in her ear asking what it was. Celia shrugged to show she didn't know. "Without further ado, I give you—" He pulled the cloth off the box. "The Lovejoy Magic Wand Flute Necklace!"

CHAPTER THIRTY-FOUR

*T*hat night at dinner, her father was still talking about his new invention. "I wish you had been there, Mother," he said to Grammy. "Celia was so stunned, she was speechless!" Gleefully he explained how he had noticed the flute necklace on Celia's dresser. When he realized it didn't work, he took it in to have Manuel fix it as a surprise. The very next night, he dreamt of Celia playing the flute out in the woods. "Except it wasn't just a flute!" he said. "In my dream, beautiful sparks flew out of it and the music was incredible. When I woke up, I got the idea that it could be a flute, magic wand, and necklace all in one. It's the perfect toy because it has multiple uses: musical instrument, decoration, and pretend. Manuel and I got to work on a prototype right away. It didn't take much for him to implant a computer chip that activated a light show when the flute is played. He's an electronics genius, you know."

"So what did you do with Celia's flute?" Grammy said. "You do know it was mine when I was little and I gave it to her myself?"

"Yes, I figured as much. I remembered seeing that old flute around when I was a kid," he said. "Unfortunately, I don't have it anymore. It turned out we couldn't fix it after all. And then we sawed it apart to see how it was constructed, and when we tried to weld the pieces back together it didn't work. It was the darndest thing. Good thing it was broken already, so it wasn't much of a loss." Her father looked sheepish. "Don't worry, Celia, you'll get the very first Lovejoy Magic Wand Flute Necklace that comes off the assembly line. I invented it in your honor, so that's only right."

That night when her parents came up to say good night, she told them not to turn on the nightlight. "Are you sure?" her mother asked, exchanging a look with her father.

"I'm sure," Celia said. "I don't need it anymore."

"Okay then," her mother said.

"If you change your mind, just holler," her father said after he'd adjusted the covers around her shoulders. They each gave her a kiss.

When they left the room, Celia heard her mother say with a sigh, "She's growing up so fast. Soon enough she won't want us to tuck her in anymore either."

After they'd gone downstairs, she got up and tiptoed outside onto the balcony. Leaning over the railing, she called out softly, "Mira, the flute is gone."

From off in the distance she heard, "It doesn't matter. You don't need it anymore." And then Mira said, "Go to bed, Celia. Sweet dreams."

She drifted off to sleep that night, content in knowing that she had been a brave and smart girl, outstanding in every way, as special as her grandmother, the original Celia. Because of her, the woods and her cozy house were safe from harm, and Paul and his family were the happiest they'd ever been. His mother said she couldn't believe the change in his Aunt Vicky. *Unbelievable* was the word she'd used. Yes, all was well in the world.

She remembered how Mira had said the Watchful Woods fairies were grateful to her and would be at her service if there ever was a need. Of course, there wasn't a need for magic in her life anymore.

But maybe sometime later. You could never tell.

THE END

ABOUT THE AUTHOR

 Karen McQuestion has had literary aspirations since the third grade, when her teacher read her short story out loud to the rest of the class as an example of a job well done. She has been writing ever since. She lives in Hartland, Wisconsin, with her husband and their three children.